Blue Christmas Balls

One man. Three women. Twelve days to achieve Yuletide sexual glory!

Christmas is coming and Matt Bunion is on a mission. Somehow, he's made the *huge* mistake of remaining a virgin well into his twenties - a grievous error he fully intends to rectify before the Queen's speech starts.

But it's not going to be easy...

What with strange requests to molest living room furniture, painfully inserted action figures, and an extremely festive lady of the night, Matt will be lucky to reach Boxing Day with his pride and manhood still intact.

From the best-selling author of *LOVE... FROM BOTH SIDES* comes the laugh-out-loud story of one man's quest to make this Christmas go with a bang.

By Nick Spalding:

Coronet Books

Love... From Both Sides
Love... And Sleepless Nights
Love... Under Different Skies

Notting Hill Press

Life… With No Breaks
Life… On A High
Blue Christmas Balls

Racket Publishing

Max Bloom In... The Cornerstone
Wordsmith... The Cornerstone Book 2
Spalding's Scary Shorts

Blue Christmas Balls

Nick Spalding

Chapters

Friday - 12 Days Until Christmas

MATT

I *will* have sex this Christmas.

I bloody well will.

As God is my witness, I *will* insert my John Thomas into a member of the opposite sex for the first time in my 27 years on this planet, or my name isn't Matthew Adrian Bunion.

...okay, sometimes I wish my name *wasn't* Matthew Adrian Bunion, but beggars can't be choosers.

Virgins can't be cowards either, and I've been both for far too long now.

It goes without saying that my virginity is a source of trauma to my self esteem whatever the time of year, but at Christmas that feeling is multiplied by a thousand and decorated with shiny bits of tinsel. As the Yuletide season approaches I begin to feel a cloying sense of worthlessness about not having a loved one with whom to celebrate the birth of our Lord and Saviour.

Christmas was most definitely *not* invented by someone with their virginity still intact, no matter what the Catholics choose to believe.

If it had been, we wouldn't be bombarded with images of happy couples sitting by the Christmas tree enjoying an egg nog, or walking hand-in-hand on a cold and frosty Christmas morning, with plump robins sitting in the nearest tree singing out of tune.

You just *know* that once the picture perfect moment is over, the pair of them will be up in the bedroom and licking each other's private parts quicker than you can say *God Rest Ye Merry Gentlemen*.

As far as I can tell, Christmas is all about the sex - providing you're old enough to know what the hell it is.

Being single and a virgin at this time of year is about as pleasant as having a blow torch waved across your genitals by Snowdrop The Christmas Elf.

This year therefore, I am determined to bring an end to this sorry state of affairs. I fully intend to see in the New Year safe in the knowledge that I have enjoyed carnal pursuits with at least one lady. This task will not be easy, but I am going to give it the best of British, and not give up until I am either satisfied, under arrest or dead.

The reasons for my ongoing virginity are multitudinous, but I think I've narrowed it down to a few central problems:

1. My haircut. I have the kind of hair that Stephen King could use as the inspiration for his next book. It is unruly, unkempt, thick, black and unwieldy. No matter how hard Isobel in A Cut Above tries to wrestle it into decent shape every three months, it still turns back into a morass of thick, black awfulness within five minutes of leaving the hairdressers.

It's rather like having a hair helmet. I often wish that something heavy would fall from the sky, just so I can take some benefit from having it. If a heavily concussed seagull were to drop onto my head, it would rebound off my hirsute mass with no damage done to my cranium whatsoever.

2. I am a nerd. Need proof? How about the fact I just used the words *multitudinous, unwieldy* and *hirsute* in the space of a few sentences?

My bookshelves creak with the weight of a thousand comic books. I own more science fiction box sets than the local branch of HMV. The only movie posters I allow on my walls are the Japanese versions. Ask me any question about the U.S.S Enterprise and I'll probably be able to tell you the answer - up to and including how long it is in feet. I have a life-sized statue of Howard The Duck in my bedroom - *and I have no idea why.*

I also wear glasses. Black ones with thick rims. You know the sort I'm on about. I've tried wearing the ultra thin expensive types, but they just make me look like I'm trying too hard.

3. Women terrify me. I don't know what to say around them, and have no clue what they're saying to me most of the time either. Women are just so dreadfully *complicated*. Men are easy to understand, because ninety percent of the time we are morons. Our entire lives are driven by two organs - the penis and the stomach. We either want to fuck it or eat it. Everything else is largely academic.

Women, on the other hand, are driven by the desire to overcomplicate the universe as much as possible. Evidence of this can be seen any time a woman pops out to pick up a new pair of tights. What should be a simple twenty minute drive down to Primark, ends up taking four hours - and results in an entirely new wardrobe, two parking tickets and a heated argument with a complete stranger. I simply don't understand how this is possible, and what I don't understand usually terrifies me.

Also, every time I see a nice pair of boobs my brain freezes solid. Anything with the power to make me lose control of my higher brain functions just by jiggling about a bit is to be feared and worshipped in equal measure.

4. I was raised in a Christian household. This automatically makes you likely to remain a virgin well into your twenties. The church doesn't like sex very much - unless it is conducted in a marital bed, lasts for less than five minutes, and isn't that much fun.

In case you hadn't noticed, the church doesn't want people to enjoy themselves. Happy people don't care whether there's a God or not, they're too busy being happy. This is not a state of affairs that religious organisations are content with. Miserable people are more likely to pray, come to church every Sunday, and contribute money to the upkeep of the roof. If there's one thing guaranteed to make people miserable it's being denied the opportunity to do squelchy and enjoyably sweaty things with one another.

Not a day seemed to go by when I was a lad without someone in a dog collar persuading me that sex was a dirty, shameful thing, and best avoided at all costs. I would then hand over my pocket money for the roof repairs, before going home and masturbating guiltily into a sock.

5. The Second World War. Alright, this one is a bit out of left field, I'll grant you, but it ruined my chances with Maria, the beautiful brunette from Munich who I met at university. Everything was going extremely well on our second date in the Student Union bar, until she leant over, kissed me... and my brain froze. The only way I was able to thaw it out was to start making jokes about the Third Reich. This happens whenever I am nervous. I tend to blurt out completely inappropriate things in an effort to break the tension.

Maria didn't appreciate my attempts at levity. One minute she was being more forward than Wayne Rooney, the next she was slapping me across the face and storming out of the bar, screaming that her grandfather had been killed at Dresden.

6. My surname is fucking *Bunion*.

These are the primary reasons for my intact virginity.

...the Enterprise is nine hundred feet long, by the way.

I've had near misses of course.

If nothing else, the law of averages dictate that over the course of a decade, in which a lot of social interaction takes place, there must have been *some* occasions when the prospect of getting my leg over was possible.

Take Cheryl Cornwall for instance.

Cheryl was at school and college with me, so we'd known each other for years. She was a girl of easy manner - and even easier virtue by all accounts. By the time she singled me out for attention, Cheryl had already worked her sexual way through most of the more handsome lads in our large and haphazard social group. I was strictly second tier at best, so never thought I'd get a shot. Colour me amazed then, when Cheryl decided to make me another notch on her bed post.

So it was that an eighteen year old (and very inebriated) Matthew Bunion was led down to the bottom of the beer garden in The Ferry Boatman pub one warm Spring evening. At the back of the garden was a large privet hedge, which provided ample seclusion and concealment. Legend has it that this was one of Cheryl Cornwall's favourite places for a bit of outdoor conjugality - and I was to be her latest conquest there.

With a beating heart and unsteady gait, I stumbled behind the hedge in the wake of Cheryl's eye watering perfume.

'I've always fancied you,' Cheryl told me, as she spat out her gum.

'Have you?' I responded in disbelief.

'Yeah. You've got nice eyes,' she said, unbuttoning her shirt to reveal the most glorious boobs I'd ever seen. This caused my brain to freeze faster than the last ice age. 'Now come here,' Cheryl ordered, fully intent on having me for breakfast. One of her hands went around my neck and the other expertly snaked its way southwards. This was to be an experience I - and my penis - would never forget!

Three minutes later I stumbled shame-faced out of the privet hedge, having ejaculated in my jeans long before Cheryl had the chance to get the old fella out and pop him in her mouth.

It was the rubbing, you see. Cheryl was very good at it, both in terms of speed and strength.

Once her hand went to my crotch and started to massage my genitals it was only a matter of time before I climaxed. It shouldn't be possible for a drunk eighteen year old girl to give you a better wank behind a hedge and through your jeans than you can achieve on your own and naked with a bottle of baby oil, but Cheryl managed it nonetheless.

It was a miracle I managed to hold off my orgasm for a whole three minutes.

Cheryl was very nice about the whole thing, to give her some credit. 'Don't worry about it, Matt,' she said in a slur, as we walked back to the pub and our friends. 'I'll just tell them I sucked you off for a while... and it was really big.'

I could have cried. This was an act of charity the likes of which I have never experienced since. Cheryl could quite easily have made me a laughing stock, but kindly chose to keep my dignity intact.

The last I heard of her she was running in the local council elections. I can't help thinking that if she ever became Prime Minister, the country would be far better off.

If Cheryl Cornwall was a kind hearted human being, then Amanda Petrovoska was a she-demon from Hell.

The daughter of a Polish used car salesman, Amanda brought poor Matt Bunion into her web of manipulation and treachery six years ago.

I was working as the junior webmaster for a local I.T firm at the time, and Amanda was one of the sales staff. She took a liking to me over the water cooler one day, dooming me for the next two years of my life. Her husky Eastern European accent and equally Eastern European good looks assured her total dominance over me the second I agreed to go out on a date with her.

Don't get me wrong, the first few weeks were wonderful. There was kissing, there was fondling, there was rubbing. Not Cheryl Cornwall quality rubbing it has to be said, but rubbing none the less.

There was even the chance to play with a pair of naked breasts on the occasion when Amanda Petrovoska allowed it.

All in all, for those first few weeks, I was a happy man - alternating between sessions of what the previous generation would call *heavy petting*, and feverish masturbation alone in my flat, imagining what disgusting antics I would get up to with Amanda once she let me go all the way with her.

Sadly, Amanda was what you'd politely call *sexually chaste*, and what you'd impolitely call a *prick tease*.

'Not yet Matt,' she'd say for the umpteenth time, pulling her skirt back down.

'Then when?' I'd ask distraught, zipping my jeans back up over an engorged and unhappy penis.

'Soon. I just need it to be the right time. You understand, don't you?'

Needless to say, the right time turned out to be *never*. No matter how much cajoling and persuasive argument I employed, Amanda never gave up the goods. At first she put this down to not wanting to rush things, then she put it down to wanting to make sure she was in love with me before having sex, and *then* she decided she didn't want to do it until after we were married. It was a nightmare.

Not only that, she was even unprepared to take pity on me and offer a bit of light hand relief, to at least tide me over. My groin was a complete no-go zone as far as Amanda was concerned.

Can you imagine how blue my balls were?

Bluer than the deepest ocean, my friend. Bluer than the clearest summer sky.

I should have finished my frustrating relationship with Amanda once it had become clear that she was stringing me along, but you have to appreciate how husky that Eastern European accent was, and how good those Eastern European looks truly were. No matter how frustrated I became, and no matter how blue my testicles glowed in the dark, I still let Amanda Petrovoska lead me around by the penis... for a full *two years*.

For forty eight months I fantasised over just *seeing* her vagina, let alone inserting anything into it. No-one should be forced to think about another person's crotch for two years. It's just not fair. And yet, Amanda was willing to allow this state of affairs to go on for as long as she deemed fit.

The endless frustration and torment eventually came to an end when I found out Amanda was fucking one of the mechanics who worked for her father's car business.

Anyone else on the planet would have been entirely unsurprised by this turn of events, but when your testicles are the same shade as the cast of Avatar, your ability to think straight is severely hampered. So much so that one of the most embarrassing moments of my life occurred the day I found out about Amanda's treachery from her friend Gretchen.

I went to confront Amanda at her father's garage, where she was now working as the admin secretary. I pleaded with her to come out of the office and onto the forecourt, with the tears already brimming in my eyes.

What followed was extremely unpleasant. I ended up shouting at the top of my voice, and crying my eyes out standing between a 54 plate Ford Ka and a 56 plate Renault Clio. Anyone passing by would have thought I really had something against small hatchbacks.

Amanda didn't try to deny the fact that Grant the six foot mechanic had been up her on a regular basis. 'He's just more of a man than you Matt,' she said, looking away with her arms folded.

'What the fuck does that mean?' I wailed.

'He doesn't mess me about Matt. He made love to me straight away. You're too timid.'

'Too timid?! You kept saying you didn't want to!'

Amanda sniffed. 'It's not my fault if you can't take control of a situation,' she said and flounced off back to the office, leaving me mouth agape and bug-eyed.

I would have followed to give her a real piece of my mind, but I could see her father Yuri giving me the stink eye from over a row of used BMWs, and thought better of it. I was pretty sure Yuri wasn't a member of the European mafia, but I wasn't prepared to risk it. I sloped away with my tail between my legs, and never saw Amanda Petrovoska again... thank Christ.

Amanda's effect on my love life continued far past the actual end of my masochistic relationship with her. I was so profoundly damaged by the whole thing that the idea of trying to find another girl scared the willies out of me. And so began a life of singledom that has been my sorry existence for the past *four* years.

Initially, this suited me just fine. Avoiding vaginas became my hobby, thanks to the horror of Amanda Petrovoska, and for a good eighteen months I was pretty damn happy being young, free and single.

Being young, free and single has a shelf life though.

For some it can stay fresh for years, for others it can go rotten in a matter of weeks. It reached its sell by date for me after about a year and a half.

As far as the outside world was concerned I was still delighted with my singularity, but inside I was starting to feel the twist of loneliness. It didn't help that quite a few of my friends were beginning to pair off at this stage - the more socially adept ones anyway. The mid-twenties is a natural time to stop gallivanting around with a series of casual partners and get into something more serious - which is precisely what my friends were now doing. This left me high, dry and thoroughly miserable.

For *two years*.

But no more. The challenge is set.

I *will* have sex this Christmas.

By hook or by crook, I will woo a lady and bed her in time for the festive season, or, as previously stated, my name's not Matthew Adrian *fucking* Bunion!

Monday - 9 Days Until Christmas

TARA

Tara is a woman I'd never have met, were it not for the miracle that is the online dating industry. Our paths would simply have never crossed otherwise.

This is the internet's greatest gift to us, and also its greatest curse. It gives us the chance to communicate with a lot of people we couldn't before... whether we should do or not.

For every long lost brother and sister it reunites, it also increases the chances of the average 14 year old girl coming into contact with Jon, the 46 year old youth leader, who likes to pretend he's 16 in the chat forums, and is looking at a ten to fifteen stretch once the constabulary catches up with him.

I bumped into Tara - electronically speaking - on a free dating site called *FishInTheSea.com*. While I'm aware that there are many pay sites out there offering dating opportunities, I am neither wealthy nor inclined enough to use them. *FishInTheSea.com* seemed like a good alternative, given that it took five minutes to set an account up, and didn't suck forty quid out of my bank account immediately upon doing so. I posted a rather neutral photo of myself ripped from my Facebook page, along with a description that was accurate but not particularly detailed, and set about my search for love among the profiles.

Of course, being a free site means that *FishInTheSea.com* is mostly populated by lunatics. Remove the barrier of payment and all the freaks like to come out and play.

It really is quite depressing how many people think it's a good idea to post pictures of their body parts when attempting to get the attention of members of the opposite sex. I realise a lot of them are just after a casual shag from other lunatics in the area, but there's got to be a better way of hauling in a prospective fuck buddy than a close-up of your labia, surely?

Clasping your erect penis so hard it turns the head an alarming shade of red, and taking a selfie of it with your iPhone can't be all that attractive to the women on *FishInTheSea.com* either, can it? Even if they are lunatics. I wouldn't imagine that the sight of a bulbous and pained looking John Thomas peeking out through a pair of tartan boxer shorts is the way to a woman's heart... or undercarriage.

Let's face it, genitals aren't the most attractive things in the world. There's a reason they are kept under cover and away from public consumption.

You wouldn't advertise your new seafood restaurant with a picture of the contents of the wheelie bin out the back. Slapping up a picture of your junk to advertise how much of a catch you are is much the same thing, as far as I'm concerned.

When the lunatics aren't providing pictures that wouldn't look out of place in a medical text book, they spend a lot of time in their descriptions trying to convince others that they are not, in fact, lunatics.

This fails of course. It's easy to spot the maniacs from a mile off.

Take Tracy's profile for instance. Everything sounds normal and above board to start off with.

'*Hi! I'm Tracy!*' the blurb starts, giving no indication of the horrors to come. '*I like to have fun! and stay up all night talking!*' it continues. Tracy may show a lack of decent grammar and a penchant for the overuse of an exclamation mark, but so far there's nothing too out of the ordinary.

The next couple of paragraphs talk about her job, her family, and whether she likes cats or dogs (it's always one or the other - stoats and bearded lizards don't get a look in) and continues in the style of a sane and well adjusted human being.

It's around paragraph three that things start to go downhill. Lunatics can only mask their lunacy for so long it seems. About 250 words is the maximum in my experience.

'*I love sausages!*' Tracy continues. This may at first appear to be perfectly reasonable. Sausages are a staple of western society. Food is an important part of life, and it's nice to know what a prospective date likes to stick in her mouth on a regular basis. With Tracy, it's sausages. All fair enough.

At this point, a rational person would now move on to talk about what other foods they enjoy. They might add a little information on what drink they like to consume as well - red wine or light beer, for instance.

Not Tracy though. Tracy is not done with the sausages. Not by a long chalk.

My favourites are good British makes like Cumberland and Cambridge, she tells us, *but I also love Chorizo, Polish and Bologna!* Okay, so slightly more information than I really need on her sausage preferences, but still not indicative of severe mental problems.

I hate Lincolnshire sausages though. I really fucking *hate them.* Oh dear, all is not right in Tracy's sausagey world it appears. We have discovered her arch nemesis. *They taste of sick. And when they're raw look horrible too. Like the way my cat's skin looked after she'd died.*

And there we have it. The full blown lunacy emerges at last.

Lunatics may start by telling you how much they love to have fun and take walks in the country, but by the time paragraph five rolls around you've had your first mention of a dead pet, and the dawning realisation that you're reading the ramblings of a mental patient.

Tracy then continues her diatribe against the humble Lincolnshire sausage for a further *three* paragraphs, before moving on to talk about how much she loves Bratwurst.

Really, *really* loves Bratwurst.

'It's the best sausage in the world!!!' she tells me - with three exclamation marks, no less. *'There's nothing I like to do more than eat a Bratwurst every single day!!!'*

Tracy has written the word 'eat' but I am one thousand percent sure that what she really means is 'insert'.

Poor old sausage obsessed Tracy is just one example of the selection of freaks and geeks you'll find on your average free dating site. Even if you're happily married, I thoroughly recommend a constructive hour spent wading through some of the profiles you'll find on one. If nothing else, it'll make you really fucking glad you're wearing that gold band on your finger.

Given the mental instability of most of the women I discovered while browsing *FishInTheSea.com*, it was something of a miracle when I found Tara in the sea of lunacy I was nearly drowning in.

I was immediately drawn to her picture. Partly because there were no genitals, boobs or other inappropriate body parts in sight, and partly because her broad smile was electric - even in the confines of a small thumbnail image.

Owner of a neat blonde bob and sparkling blue eyes, Tara looked like the kind of girl that wouldn't hurt a fly - or insert pork products into any of her orifices.

Her description backed up this first impression. Like most, she loved to have fun and preferred dogs to cats, but by the time I reached the last paragraph I had been given no indication that she was harbouring any psychopathic tendencies. I re-read the profile description several times to make sure I hadn't missed anything - like a veiled reference to the beauty of human taxidermy - but still nothing struck me as out of the ordinary.

By all accounts, Tara seemed like a nice, intelligent, normal girl.

I was immediately and comprehensively suspicious. So much so that I had absolutely no intention of getting in touch with her. But then I remembered that I was still a virgin, and likely to remain so if I didn't take a risk.

I wrote Tara a short and succinct message to see if she'd like to chat with me, and emailed it to her with my heart racing.

I then heard nothing for three days, so I naturally assumed she'd taken one look at my picture, vomited all over her keyboard, and clicked through to the next guy's profile.

On the third day however - as I was looking at somebody called *LadyHardLove*, a sixteen stone dominatrix who promised the kind of antics that the Geneva Convention had otherwise made illegal worldwide - a message popped into my inbox from Tara. Yes, she would indeed like to chat. She thought I was very nice looking, and even complimented me on my glasses. Miracle of miracles.

Thus began an electronic back and forth that went on for a few weeks, until I eventually plucked up the courage to ask her out on a real live date. All our communication so far had suggested that Tara was a normal, well adjusted individual, so I didn't feel too terrified at the prospect of meeting her face to face.

She was also blessed with very perky breasts. I discovered this when we started to trade photos, and she sent me one of her on holiday in Rimini. I'm not saying that perky breasts are necessarily the best indicator of a woman's sanity level, but it can't hurt to have them, can it? If I am going to be scalped in a bathtub, I'd rather it was done by someone with good looking boobs.

Tara said yes to the date, and a few days later we met at the Costa coffee shop next to the new library building in town. Tara is an architect's assistant, and the library was a job she'd recently worked on. She seemed very keen on telling me about how she'd been instrumental in the design of the glass front entrance. I thought it looked a bit like a large, shiny greenhouse, but kept my mouth shut, because nobody likes to hear criticism on a first date.

We had something in common at least. As a web designer, I could appreciate the time and effort that went into building the glass monstrosity sat alongside us, even if I didn't actually like the end result much.

All in all, as first dates go, it went quite well. As did the wank I had that evening thinking about those perky breasts.

The second date was equally acceptable. In fact, I'd go so far as to say it was the best second date I'd ever had. It certainly beat getting slapped by an irate German after I'd made a crack about Hitler's moustache.

Tara chose the site for the second date too, a sure sign that this was a woman who liked to be in charge. I had no problem with this of course, being that I once spent two years being ordered around by a husky Eastern European accent.

Tara took me for a meal in a rather swanky restaurant called *De Rigueur*. It was one of those contemporary places, with a limited menu and exorbitant prices. Rather than the classic restaurant decor of soft lighting, hard wooden chairs, and easy listening music playing in the background, this place was all about chrome, glass, arc sodium and ambient techno.

The lights bounced off so many bright and shiny surfaces I wish I'd worn my prescription sunglasses. Still, I enjoyed my biscuit sized beef burger and the small handful of parsnip chips that came with it. Both had more pretentious names than that on the menu, but they were in French and I've already forgotten what they were.

The evening was capped off delightfully with a walk by the canal that ended in a snogging session initiated by Tara under a bridge. She even massaged my penis for a bit. I was prepared for it this time thanks to Cheryl Cornwall, and managed to keep things under control until we parted company half an hour later.

Driving home was slightly difficult, given that my erection kept getting in the way of the steering wheel, but other than that the date was a complete success in my book.

It obviously was for Tara as well as she rang me the next morning.

'I had a great time last night,' she said.

'Thanks. I had fun too. Though the parsnip chips kept repeating on me.'

'You're a funny guy Matt.'

'Er... thanks.'

'Want to see me again? I'm choc-a-block with Christmas parties this week, but I'm free Wednesday, if you are?'

'Yes! Yes!' I replied a little too quickly, and definitely too loudly. 'Wednesday would be good for me.'

'Great. I'll call you about a time and place in the afternoon.'

'Okay.'

'And Matt?'

'Yeah?'

'I can't stop thinking about what we did under the bridge.' Tara's voice was now a barely audible, but incredibly sexy whisper. 'I'd love to take things even further with you...'

'Hmnmnm.'

'See you on Wednesday!'

'Hnnerr mnermn.'

That was three days ago.

Today is Wednesday.

Oh, the terror.

While Tara didn't quite come out and say that she was ready, willing and able to have sex with me, that conversation has led me to believe that it is definitely on the cards. I may know as much about women as I do the surface of Jupiter, but even I can understand a heavy handed hint when I hear one.

For the first time since Amanda bloody Petrovoska and her permanently camouflaged vagina, I have a very good chance of getting laid. And what's more, the woman in question is attractive, sane, has 20-20 vision, and isn't on the run from any law enforcement agencies (as far as I know).

If I can just manage to play things cool and not embarrass myself, I might just be on to a winner here.

***

Hmmmm.

The date started well - which may come as something of a surprise when I reveal that we went ice skating.

I am six foot one, gangly, and the owner of insane hair, thick spectacles, and the aforementioned Howard The Duck statue, so the very fact that I agreed to go ice skating in the first place should speak volumes about my desire to see Tara naked.

Men like me are not cut out for such graceful pursuits. We simply aren't packaged correctly for it. Ice skating requires a certain amount of innate poise, and I am sadly lacking in that department. It's entirely possible for me to fall over while walking across soft grass in a pair of sensible walking boots, so you can only imagine the difficulties encountered when slippery ice and sharp metal blades are introduced into the equation.

'You're doing very well!' Tara calls out to me as I grip the barrier around the edge of the ice rink for dear life. Tara is being very generous. I'd only be doing *very well* if it was a competition to see how many times you can fall down in the space of five minutes without breaking any bones. My arse will be black and blue in the morning.

I wave at her with one shaky hand and attempt to scuttle another three feet along the ice, trying to avoid being pole-axed by a passing seven year old. My goal is to complete at least one complete circuit of the ice rink before our time is up. I only have half an hour, so it's going to be a close run thing.

Tara offers me words of encouragement every time she goes past. This doesn't help matters one little bit. Just as I'm at the point of quite rightly throwing in the towel, she skates past with a smile and wave - and I get another look at her peachy bottom for the umpteenth time. This encourages my penis to continue with the stumbling attempt to complete the circle. My legs, arse, arms and rib cage want to escape this frozen, awkward hell as quickly as possible, in favour of a nice cup of hot chocolate from the vending machine, but I am a man, and therefore the penis always holds the deciding vote.

Nevertheless, by the time a strident klaxon sounds to tell us all to get off the ice and let the next group on, I have indeed made it back round to my starting position.

Tara skates up to me with a breathless look of contentment on her face. 'That was lovely!' she exclaims.

'Yes it was!' I lie enthusiastically.

'Thanks for coming with me,' she adds as she helps me back on to the relative safety of the concrete floor. I'm still wearing the ridiculous ice skates so could quite easily snap an ankle, but at least I'm back on dry land, where the chances of that happening have diminished considerably.

'No worries. Happy to come along.'

We both sit down on a nearby bench and start to unlace our boots. 'I've always loved skating,' Tara tells me, looking back at the ice with a smile. 'Gliding along on a smooth surface like that always gives me a thrill.'

Without seeming to think about it, one of Tara's hands snakes its way between my legs and gives me a gentle rub. My penis starts to scream '*I told you so!*' to the rest of my body at the top of its voice.

It appears that the thirty minutes of painful, awkward stumbling may be about to pay dividends.

'I need to warm up,' Tara says, slipping her shoes back on. 'My place is only about five minutes away. Shall we go back there and I'll make us coffee?'

'Sounds like a great idea to me!' I nod energetically. At the back of my mind I'm wondering how I can donate some money to the people who run the ice rink.

I follow Tara back to her house, trying to keep my combination of excitement and apprehension under some kind of control.

This is *it*. This is the night it finally happens!

...potentially anyway.

I'm not counting my chickens until they've hatched. Cheryl, Maria and Amanda have well and truly taught me that lesson over the years.

Tara's top floor flat is exquisite. Part of a quayside apartment complex at the edge of the city, it's brand new, shiny and located conveniently for all the needs of a young professional. You could stand on her balcony and spit on at least four coffee shops, two tapas bars, and a vegan food shop.

I am eternally glad I didn't suggest going back to my place. I live in the ground floor flat of a converted Victorian pile that was probably old fashioned ten minutes after they'd hammered in the last roof tile. If my place could speak it would call everyone a bastard as they walked past.

I park my rusty Volkswagen Golf in the vast underground car park below Tara's apartment complex. I feel shame and embarrassment for my car as I leave it surrounded by other vehicles all at least eight years younger and ten times cleaner. If I come back to find it has leaked oil all over itself in humiliation, I won't be surprised in the slightest.

Tara offers me a speculative smile as we ride the elevator to the top floor. She then plants a soft, seductive kiss on my lips just before the doors open. As we walk along the corridor to her front door I have to loosen my shirt collar a bit as I've suddenly come over very hot and bothered.

'Nice pad,' I say as she shows me in.

This is something of an understatement. Tara's flat is *amazing*. For starters it's a broad open plan expanse, artfully strewn with the kind of bespoke furniture that would explode in disgust if it got within a hundred feet of an Ikea catalogue. The floor is a rich, glistening hard wood, stained to a glorious caramel colour. I want to bend down and give it a lick. The white and black kitchen gleams like it's just leapt from the pages of a catalogue, and the living area is dominated by both a fifty inch flat screen TV fixed to the wall, and a large glass coffee table that is roughly the same size as my bedroom. Surrounding it are two retro looking Chesterfield sofas, which should look completely out of place but don't, as they provide a pleasing contrast to all the modern stuff.

'*Really* nice pad,' I repeat as Tara plays with the coffee machine built into one of the kitchen cabinets.

'Thanks. The rent is a bitch, but with views like that, who can complain?'

I have to agree as I walk over to the bank of triple glazed windows that comprise the entire southern wall of the flat. Even though it's night time, I can still look down at the vast quayside complex below us, and beyond it out over the dark channel waters, where the occasional ship can be identified by its running lights.

It is at this moment I appreciate for the first time how much trouble I am in. Tara is obviously used to the finer things in life. Her job must be very well paid to afford this place, that much is certain. Quite why she needed to go on *FishInTheSea.com* is baffling.

And here I am, a gangly virgin, standing in her living room and looking out at the kind of view my salary couldn't afford if I worked non-stop for the next eight centuries.

'Latte or cappuccino?' Tara asks.

'Er... latte?' I suggest, even though my coffee drinking exploits usually begin and end with an occasional mug of Gold Blend.

Tara goes to work on the drink and I look back out of the expansive window as the sound of a dinosaur clearing its throat echoes through the flat. I hope the coffee tastes better than it sounds to make.

'Here you go,' Tara says a few minutes later, handing me a tall glass full of milky coffee. 'Amazing view, isn't it?' she says, sipping her own latte.

'Yes indeed. I bet you can see for miles in the daytime.'

'Sometimes I like to be a nosy neighbour,' she tells me with a smirk. 'You can look into a lot of the windows from here.' Tara leans one hand against the cool triple glazing and peers out at the shorter apartment blocks surrounding hers. 'It's amazing how many times I've caught people fucking.'

She says this with a thrill in her voice that puts a lump in both my throat and jeans.

'Give me that,' Tara says, having noticed the expression on my face. She whisks the coffee away from my hands and puts it on the floor. Her arms go around my neck and pull my head down, so she can give me a very aggressive kiss on the lips. 'Now,' she says, her eyelids heavy. 'Let's give my neighbours something to talk about.'

We're in a block of flats at least five stories higher than those surrounding us, so unless her neighbours are Spider-man and Superman I don't think we'll be giving anyone a show, but I choose not to bring this rather asinine point up. Instead I do as I am told. I'd rather sit on a comfy couch and go about this in a more dignified manner, but if this is what Tara likes, then I'm not going to complain.

I'm frankly glad to get some sort of direction. I'm extremely nervous now, and wouldn't be able to take the lead if you paid me vast sums of money and let me have six months rehearsal.

'Pin me against the window Matt,' Tara demands. This is a girl who likes things a bit rough it seems. I hold her arms against the window and stick my tongue down her throat in the accepted manner. Every time I increase the pressure on her arms she moans, indicating that I'm definitely doing what she wants.

'We're going to break the window in a minute,' I say to her.

'Not a chance,' she replies breathlessly. 'These are heat tempered and toughened with a bi-weave laminate. They're the best... *oh my God*... the best in the business.' One arm breaks free of my grip and grabs my crotch. 'You can't get better glass Matt,' she tells me.

Tara sounds like a UPVC salesman, but I'm not making an issue of it as my flies are now being unzipped.

Quick as a flash my jeans and boxer shorts are down around my ankles and I'm spun around so I'm now the one up against the window. My naked arse slams into the cold glass, eliciting a squawk of surprise.

'Feels great, doesn't it?' Tara gasps. 'The glass against your skin?'

She doesn't give me a chance to reply as now her hand grips my penis, causing all coherent thought to disappear into the ether. Her other hand pushes my pelvis harder against the window, and Tara starts to administer a hand job that forces me to close my eyes and think about my grandmother naked.

I MUST not orgasm too early tonight. There is sex to be had in these four walls, and I'm not going to let anything come between me and it - especially my over-excitable penis.

The cold glass is helping, it has to be said. As is the strange squeaking noise my backside makes against it every time I shift position slightly. It's a little difficult to ejaculate prematurely when your bottom is being used as a giant squeegee mop.

Tara kisses me fiercely on the lips again and then steps away. 'Let's get naked,' she says and unzips her own jeans.

'Okay!' I bellow and wrench my sweater and shirt off in a micro-second. This gives me chance to watch Tara slide her lacy underwear down her legs and stand up straight again. Heat tempered and toughened with a bi-weave laminate these windows may be, but if I choose to spin round right now, my hard-on is so enormous it would surely shatter the glass with no effort whatsoever.

Tara grabs my cock once again and leans in close. 'Want to do something a bit kinky?' she whispers in my ear.

Now, *kinky* is a word that conjures up all kinds of images - not all of them good.

Kinky can just mean a little light bondage with scarves and such, but it can also mean having a hairy dwarf dressed as Hitler suspended on a bungee cord above your head, with his bowels open.

You can therefore understand it when I'm a little unsure how to respond to Tara's request.

'Trust me,' she says with a smile, sensing my uncertainty.

'Okay...' I respond, praying that a midget isn't about to jump out of a kitchen cupboard waving a dildo.

'Come with me,' she whispers and leads me to the living area.

Tara then sinks to her knees, leading me to believe I'm about to get a blow job. *Woo hoo!*

I'm wrong though, as now Tara does something totally unexpected. She crawls under the enormous glass coffee table.

'Er...' I start to say, but don't really know what to follow it up with. Is she looking for something? Perhaps she's spotted a pound coin?

Tara positions herself on her back beneath the coffee table and looks up at me through the glass. 'Lie down on it for me,' she says.

'What?' I ask, non-plussed. What the hell is going on here?

'Lie down on the coffee table Matt,' she repeats.

'But... but *why*?'

She cocks her head to one side. 'Because I want you to. Because it'll be hot.'

'No it won't, it looks freezing cold to me.'

'Please Matt.' Tara bats her eyelids, and one hand slides down her stomach. 'You want me to be happy, don't you?' The hand keeps going.

'Yes. Yes, I want you to be happy,' I reply, not able to take my eyes off what she's now doing with her fingers.

'Go on then... just lie out flat on it for me.'

This is officially the weirdest request I've ever been given, but this is also the closest I've been to sex for a *very* long time. If I'm going to get over the virginity hump, I'll just have to suck it up and go for it. Nothing ventured, nothing gained.

I gasp as my bottom touches the glass surface, but I lower myself fully onto the table and put my head back, wondering what's supposed to happen next.

'Er, Matt...' Tara ventures.

'Yep?'

'I meant the other way around, so you're facing me. All I can see at the moment is your squashed arse.'

'Ah... gotcha.'

I turn around and gently lower myself again, grimacing as my still engorged penis rests against the cool surface.

So now we are facing each other, with about half an inch of glass the only thing separating our naked bodies. If Tara is worried about a decent form of contraception, then this is about as efficient as it gets.

'So, you... you like this kind of thing do you?' I ask hesitantly.

Tara's eyelids flutter as her fingers continue to have fun downstairs. 'Oh God yes. It's the glass. The feel of it, the look of it... ' She trails off and I watch as her other hand presses against the underside of the coffee table right underneath my cock.

'So... do I do anything?' I ask in understandable curiosity.

'Yeah, yeah. Move around a bit.'

'What?'

'Move around. I want to see your skin move against the glass.'

'How do you mean? Up and down or side to side?'

'Up and down,' Tara moans. 'Let me see you do it.'

The things we do to get laid, eh?

I grab the edge of the huge table and start to pull myself forward. A high pitched and drawn out squeal fills the flat as I drag my flesh across the glassy surface.

SSQQUUEEAALL

'And back down again!' Tara cries. 'Keep going!'

SSSQQQUUUEEEAAALLL

'Oh God yes!'

I came here tonight in hopes of having sex with an attractive woman, but have ended up sexually molesting an item of living room furniture. Not even a good one, either. At least humping the shit out of the couch would have been warm and comfortable.

While I am now having about as much fun as I did the last time I went to the dentist, Tara is in the throes of absolute sexual pleasure. Her fingers are going ten to the dozen down there. If I don't make some kind of move soon, she's going to be all finished up before I so much as get a chance to introduce my erect penis into the equation.

'Are we going to have sex Tara?' I ask forlornly.

'We are having sex!' she wails. 'Keep sliding about!'

SSSSQQQQUUUUEEEEAAAALLLLL

'Oh fuck me, that's so good!'

SSSSSQQQQQUUUUUEEEEEAAAAALLLL

'Faster Matt!'

'I don't want to! I feel stupid and I'm getting friction burns!'

'Do it and I'll let you fuck me in the ass afterwards!'

*SSSSSSQQQQQQUUUUUUUEEEEEEEAAAAAALLL
LLL*

'Oh God... that's it... that's it...'

*SSSSSSSQQQQQQQUUUUUUUUUEEEEEEEEAAA
AAAA -* **CRACK**!

It is the sound of inevitability.

It is the sound of Armageddon.

It is the sound of the coffee table about to give way.

I instantly go wide-eyed with mind-numbing terror. It takes a second longer for Tara's expression to change from one of orgasmic delight to sudden, horrific understanding.

We both watch as a crack speeds across the surface of the coffee table from the lower left hand corner to the upper right.

If I don't do something very, *very* quickly, there will be a degree of nastiness in my immediate future that could border on life threatening.

Tara's brain is sending her the same message, and she immediately starts to back her way out from under the table on her elbows.

I have two choices. I can either scramble backwards to alleviate the pressure on the cracking glass, or I can push myself forward and off the table headfirst.

Another loud and terrifying crack makes my mind up for me in a split second. I grasp the edge of the glass again and fling my body forward with all my might. Like an arthritic porpoise I shoot off the end of the coffee table with a screech of pain as the friction burns my stomach, thighs and penis.

Tara has backed out from under the table far enough so she is safe from any falling glass, but not far enough to avoid me hurtling towards her at a rate of knots. I fly off the coffee table completely and plummet towards the floor, neatly head butting her in the vagina as I do so.

Tara screams in pain and backs away from me as fast as she can. This unfortunately brings her head into contact with the wooden leg of one of her Chesterfield sofas with a dull clunk.

Fearing any more injury, Tara then instinctively curls herself up into a ball, as I roll quickly away from her like a naked ninja.

I turn swiftly to look at the coffee table and see that the crack has gotten no larger. I have staved off disaster. I may have a burned willy and seriously damaged Tara's chances of ever having children, but at least neither of us has been cut to pieces by shards of tempered glass.

I sit back on my haunches and look down at my reddened and swollen member. He's still semi-hard, bless him, despite the trauma I've put him through tonight.

Tara tentatively uncurls and rests her back against the sofa.

'I'm really sorry about that,' I tell her. 'Was it expensive?'

Tara's hand goes to the back of her head. It comes away wet with blood. 'I think... I think I need to go to casualty,' she says in a watery voice.

***

It's only a very small cut in the end. Head wounds tend to bleed a lot.

As it's a weekday, we only have to wait about half an hour in the A&E department before we're seen. This is just as well, as my poor penis is quite sore from the friction burns and is rubbing uncomfortably against my jeans whenever I shift my legs.

Tara is treated by a harassed looking female nurse in her twenties, who's long dark hair is a tangled mess thanks to what I can only assume has been a hard shift. 'How did this happen then?' she asks as she puts a single stitch in the wound.

'Just an accident at my place,' Tara responds. 'Hit my head on the arm of a couch.' It sounds like a perfectly innocent excuse, but the fact that both of us are blushing like maniacs rather indicates that more was going on than Tara is prepared to reveal.

The nurse arches one eyebrow briefly as she finishes her work. 'Okay... well, maybe be a bit more careful in future?' She gives me a look. 'Whatever it was you were doing.' I can't tell whether she thinks I'm a sexual pervert or a domestic abuser. Neither opinion is particularly good.

Tara and I leave the hospital at about midnight. I drive her back to the flat in silence.

What can you say after you've head butted a woman in the vagina? Especially one who thinks that glass is the sexiest thing on the planet.

Frankly I'll be glad to drop her off and get home as quickly as possible. Her fetish is just too weird for me. I'm desperate to lose my virginity, but not so desperate that I want to spend any time with my testicles mashed against her triple-gazing while she abuses me with a milk bottle.

Tara chooses to break the silence as she gets out of the car. 'I'm sorry things didn't work out better tonight.'

'Yeah, me too. Sorry about, you know, your coffee table and everything.'

'Don't worry.' She offers me a tired smile. 'Maybe we could go out again sometime?'

Yeah... perhaps we could go to a garden centre and you can molest me in a greenhouse.

'Er... yeah, *maybe*,' I reply, trying to keep the reluctant tone out of my voice.

It doesn't work. Tara's eyes narrow as she gets my clumsy unspoken message. 'Well, goodbye then Matt,' she says in a flat voice.

'Yeah. Goodbye Tara.' This doesn't seem quite adequate. 'I really am sorry for head butting you in the vagina.'

'It's okay,' she says and rolls her eyes. 'It's not the first time it's happened.'

———

Tara slams the car door and marches off before I get the chance to respond.

As I drive away, I can't help feeling that while I didn't get to have sex tonight, it's probably good that I didn't get further caught up in the life of a woman who's had more than one bloke administer a Glaswegian Kiss to her private parts.

Saturday - 4 Days Until Christmas

HAYLEY

Oh God, I am a worm.

A wriggling, slimy, good for nothing *worm*.

Why else would I take advantage of a long term friendship to satisfy my disgusting sexual desires?

As I've already pointed out, I am something of a nerd.

I enjoy many, *many* science fiction programs. I can tell you which comic book issue a character appears in for the first time, and I like to buy twelve inch plastic figurines of my favourite characters, which I proudly display in areas of my flat where they're not likely to be attacked by the mould.

Luckily for me, I am able to control my nerdiness well enough to function as a productive member of society - most of the time anyway. I hold down a job, take part in social activities with less nerdy friends, and can engage random people in conversation if the need arises. I more or less pass for normal 90% of the time. Okay, I wear thick black glasses, have unruly hair, and have been known to wear the odd Star Wars t-shirt now and again, but all those things can come under the umbrella of 'geek chic' and thus I am able to get away with it.

This is not the case for many of my nerd brethren. Their levels of geekiness can become so extreme that it leads to crippling social maladjustment.

Take my friend Carl for instance.

I met Carl in Forbidden Planet four years ago. We bonded over a discussion about who was sexier - The Scarlet Witch from the X-Men, or Black Canary from the Green Arrow comics.

Carl dresses like my grandfather and only goes out of the house to visit comic book shops or attend comic book conventions. If he ever breaks a limb, the paramedics will have to dress the ambulance as the Batmobile to get him to even contemplate a ride in it.

Talk to Carl about comics and you're fine. Try to engage him in a conversation about anything else and he will turn a bright shade of red, his eyes will bulge in their sockets and there's every chance he'll wet himself as some kind of half-arsed defence mechanism.

I love him to pieces, but even I have to take a step backward sometimes and regard his insanity from a safe distance.

Over the years I have come into contact with quite a few people like Carl, and have bonded with all of them quite magnificently. There's nothing quite like a mutual obsession with lightsaber technology to form the bedrock of a solid friendship.

As a social group, we don't go out much. There's the odd visit to the cinema to watch the latest blockbuster (Carl only comes if it's a comic book movie) or annual visits to the various science fiction conventions that happen around the country, but other than that, we tend to hang out in each other's houses.

This is common for most nerds. When you suffer from social awkwardness it's far better to be a homebody - and invite your fellow nerds around for a night of Pan Galactic Gargle Blasters and Romulan Ale. That way you don't have to worry about bumping into anyone who doesn't know the length of the Starship Enterprise.

Such was the case last night for my own group of spectacular geeks.

At least once a month we like to get together and play a rollicking good game of Trivial Pursuit. Not the bog-standard Genus edition though. I'm talking Star Wars Trivial Pursuit, or Lord Of The Rings Trivial Pursuit. You know... the *good stuff*.

If we get a bit bored with the Trivial Pursuit, the Monopoly comes out. I prefer the Star Trek edition, but Carl always moans until we play the Marvel Comics version instead.

We once tried to play Cluedo for the sake of variety, but it didn't feel right and we all had to go for a long lie down afterwards.

I was particularly looking forward to last night, as we were due to play Star Wars Trivial Pursuit, my own personal favourite. To commemorate the occasion I wore the brand new Boba Fett onesie I'd just bought on Amazon.

In a rather reluctant concession to the Yuletide season, I also wore the red Christmas bobble hat my Nan had knitted for me a few years ago, when she was still in control of most of her faculties.

The host of the festivities on this occasion was Hayley, the only female in our collective.

Hayley is that rarest of breeds, a woman who actively and openly enjoys science fiction. She thinks nothing of leaving the house wearing a Doctor Who t-shirt, and will happily engage anyone she meets in an animated conversation about how great an actor David Tennant is.

Hayley came into our select circle through Carl, after they met online in a sci-fi forum. Carl was enamoured with her from the first moment he laid eyes on her avatar. It was an illustration of Princess Leia in her golden bikini, holding a sonic screwdriver. Hayley is in fact a pleasant faced brunette with a pale complexion and a rather flat chest, but Carl is all about the online presence. He fell in love with her purely based on that picture... along with a shared hatred of all things Twilight.

Sadly for Carl, Hayley has never reciprocated those feelings. Partly because Carl is a borderline shut-in with a Wolverine obsession, and partly because she fancies *me*.

I know this because about six months ago we went to a Star Wars convention in Birmingham together, got drunk on cheap cider and ended up snogging next to a particularly unconvincing plastic reproduction of Jabba The Hutt. I had the presence of mind enough to detach myself from the situation before it got too out of hand. Hayley is a good friend, and I wouldn't want to ruin that relationship. Besides, it would have crushed poor Carl to know that I had stolen the love of his life.

The journey home from Birmingham on the train was fairly uncomfortable. Particularly when Hayley professed her true feelings for me in an alcoholic miasma. Rejecting someone's advances is never a pleasant business, especially when they're one of your best friends. Don't get me wrong, I would have loved to have felt the same way about her, but the spark just wasn't there for me. Perhaps I was also afraid that Carl might attack me with his stainless steel Dwarven battle axe if he found out.

The incident was more or less forgotten about after a couple of weeks, but ever since then I've caught Hayley looking at me in a strange way a few times during a Trivial Pursuit session. It's a look that speaks volumes.

I'm the last to turn up at Hayley's door this particular evening.

Boba Fett onesies are great for lounging around the house in, but they do tend to spark off conversations with acerbic taxi drivers that can go on for longer than you'd like. I just wanted to pay the bastard and run away, but he held me up for a good five minutes trying to fathom why a fully grown man would dress like a new born baby in public. I told him I suffered from clothing Tourettes Syndrome and threw a ten pound note at his baffled expression before making my escape.

Hayley answers the door to her second floor flat with a beaming smile. By startling coincidence, she is also dressed in a Boba Fett onesie.

'I can't believe you bought one too!' she squeals with delight as I walk into the hallway. 'Bounty Hunter hug!' she cries and throws her arms around me. I swear one of her hands grabs my arse as she does it, but these onesies are thick, so it's a bit hard to be sure.

'Wow. That is a coincidence,' I agree. 'Is everyone else here?' I add, in an effort to steer the conversation away from our like-minded dress sense.

'Yep. The board's set up and I've made a round of Giggling Yodas.' Hayley has become obsessed in recent weeks with sci-fi themed cocktails. The Giggling Yoda is her favourite. It looks like green slime, but mostly contains vodka. Any cocktail is fine by me as long as it mostly contains vodka.

I walk into Hayley's small lounge to be greeted by the whole gang.

'Evening Matt!' says Chinese Pete with a smile.

'You're dressed the same as Hayley!' remarks Submarine Pete from around a mouthful of Wotzits.

In a group of only seven people, it is something of a coincidence that two of us would share the same name. Even more so than two people wearing the same onesie.

One Pete works for an electronics company that outfits maritime vessels, the other Pete is half Chinese. He also works as a theatre assistant in the gynaecology department of the local hospital, but frowned upon being called Clitoris Pete, so we went with his ethnicity instead.

Munchkin gives me a wave and returns to the task of dividing Trivial Pursuit cheeses into neat piles. At five foot two, it's easy to understand where his nickname comes from. At Halloween, Munchkin always likes to dress as Lurch from The Addams Family, displaying a command of self-deprecating irony that most would find beyond them.

Last of the magnificent seven is Simon Boring, a man of skinny physique and pointed nose. Simon's surname is not in fact Boring, it's Boreman. He is an avid fan of Frank Herbert's Dune though. The rest of us all agree that Frank Herbert's seminal science fiction saga is the dullest thing ever committed to the page - hence Simon's hilariously altered surname.

'You're late Bunion,' Simon Boring says with narrowed eyes, obviously impatient to get on with the game.

I do not need a silly nickname. Given that my surname is Bunion, I already have one built in.

'Sorry gang,' I apologise. 'I got waylaid by a taxi driver who took exception to my attire.'

'Copying Hayley are we?' Carl points out in a tart voice.

'No! I only got mine today, and we haven't spoken!' Hayley answers. She puts two fingers to her temples. 'It's like we're... you know... joined psychically or something.'

This elicits a dark look from Carl, an awkward look from me, and raised eyebrows from the rest of the crew, who can tell Hayley fancies me as easily as I can.

'Sit down Matt,' she says, patting one of her rather threadbare armchairs. 'I'll bring the cocktails out and we can get started.'

'Okay.' I plonk myself down next to Munchkin and help myself to the bowl of peanuts on the coffee table. This table is made of sturdy oak, so no matter what else happens tonight, I won't be sliding myself up and down on it for fear of getting splinters.

Hayley comes back into the living room with a tray of Giggling Yodas. She lets us all take one, and then sits herself on the arm of the chair I'm sat in. I pointedly don't look at Carl.

'Right then, you wretched hive of scum and villainy,' Munchkin intones, in an awful impression of Sir Alec Guinness. 'Let's get on with the game!'

Playing Star Wars Trivial Pursuit is not like playing normal Trivial Pursuit. There tends to be a lot of arguments. These usually erupt when an answer to a question is deemed inaccurate. *'But R2-5Q doesn't appear in A New Hope! Only in Empire Strikes Back! The answer is wrong!'* is a fairly typical pronouncement, which invariably leads to a heated debate over how many R2 units appear in the trilogy, and when.

We also tend to fly off on tangents that have nothing to do with the question at all. I distinctly remember being asked one about Gandalf's magic staff that eventually devolved into an argument about whether it's possible to genetically engineer square honeydew melons. I couldn't back track my way through that conversation if you put a gun to my head.

Needless to say, our games of Trivial Pursuit go on for quite a while...

It's one in the morning before Hayley yawns expansively and puts a decisive end to proceedings. 'That's enough guys. Carl won an hour ago. Let's just say Chinese Pete and Matt tied for second and leave it at that.'

'Alright,' Chinese Pete says and stretches. 'But I want it put on record that Simon Boring is wrong to say that the Falcon's heat shielding is inadequate to prevent burn up on re-entry into a planet's atmosphere.'

'But it is! You can tell by the schematics that it would never - '

'Enough!' Carl snaps. 'Hayley says we're done, so let's leave this discussion for another time.'

'Yeah, we should let her... let her get to shleep,' I slur. I've had four Giggling Yodas and a can of Stella tonight. This is way in excess of my usual levels of alcohol consumption. I am, in no uncertain terms, pretty damn wankered.

Carl, who is teetotal to the extreme, fishes out the keys of his ancient Fiat Cinquecento. 'I can give three of you a lift. There isn't enough room for four.'

'I've got my bike,' Munchkin says.

This leaves the two Petes, Simon Boring and me needing a lift.

There is a moment of exquisite tension. None of us want to be the one to make the supreme sacrifice and have to pay for a taxi.

A quick bit of mental calculation - quick for someone who's consumed four Giggling Yodas - tells me that I live the closest of the four of us. This is a fact that the others are aware of as well.

I can choose to handle this situation in one of two ways. Either we get into a heated debate over who should dip out on a free lift, with me eventually losing the argument given that I only live a ten minute drive away - or I can fall on my sword, earn the respect and admiration of all concerned, and call in the debt at a later date. As it's one in the morning and I'm as pissed as a fart, I elect for the latter option. 'I'll get a cab guys, don't worry about it,' I say magnanimously.

The looks of relief are quite palpable.

Within a few minutes Hayley is closing the door on the rest of the gang, and I'm pulling out my phone to call the local taxi firm.

My fingers are hovering over the first digit when Satan decides to have a conversation with me.

'**Hello Matthew**,' the evil one says.

'Satan?'

'**Yes Matthew. It is I. The Accursed One. The Fallen Angel. The Monster From The Pit.**'

'What do you want with me?'

'**Well Matthew, as I was busy slouching towards Bethlehem I couldn't help notice that you are now alone in Hayley's flat with her.**'

'Yes. What about it?'

'**Hayley fancies you Matthew. If you want to, you could quite easily get into her knickers tonight.**'

'No Satan! I couldn't! Hayley is my friend and I can't take advantage of her like that.'

'Really? This is a golden opportunity to lose your virginity and you're not going to take it?'

'I said I can't do that to her!'

'Yes you can Matthew. You can, or you can stay a loveless virgin for the rest of your life. Here's your chance. Take it!'

I look up at Hayley as she busies herself with dumping the detritus of the evening into a black bin liner. In her onesie, with her hair dishevelled from a night of drinking Giggling Yodas and playing Trivial Pursuit, she doesn't exactly look like every man's sexual fantasy, if I'm being honest.

As Satan points out though, I am currently alone in a flat with a girl who has wanted me to make a move for months. If I made the effort, I could be thrusting my way to full manhood in a matter of minutes.

In my jeans, my penis twitches, offering his contribution to the debate - one which tips me over the edge into utter bastard territory.

I lock my phone and put it back in my pocket. 'Do you want a hand with that?' I ask Hayley. I can almost hear the hosts of Heaven heave a collective sigh of disgust as I do.

'Yeah okay. Thanks,' Hayley replies with a tired smile. 'Good night, wasn't it?'

'It was! Always is when we get together,' I reply as I dump several empty Doritos packets into the bin liner. Hayley tucks an errant strand of hair behind one ear and yawns.

This is it then... my last chance to do the right thing and leave.

Satan doesn't let me take it. 'I thought you looked really cute tonight in your onesie,' I tell Hayley. 'You wear it much better than me.'

Hayley beams with pleasure, and a small piece of my soul dies. 'Thanks Matt!' she says. 'You looked nice in yours too.'

Sigh.

In for a penny, in for a pound.

'I er... wouldn't mind seeing you out of it too,' I mumble.

Hayley immediately goes redder than Magneto's helmet. 'I... I didn't think you liked me that way Matt,' she stammers.

'Yeah, I do Hayley. I *really* do.'

You utter, utter bastard Bunion. You'll rot for this.

If I was sober, I might be able to resist this turn to the Darkside, but in my current inebriated condition, Satan and my penis hold full sway.

I move closer to Hayley and plant a kiss on her lips. 'I'd like to stay with you tonight... if you want me too,' I say to her and stroke her arm.

Hayley looks away and starts to nibble a fingernail. 'I don't know Matt. This is very sudden. What about what you said in Birmingham?'

'Forget what I said then. I was wrong.' I put my arms around her. 'I really want you Hayley.'

'I didn't think you felt anything for me. I thought you just wanted to be friends.'

I don't feel anything for you Hayley, you're absolutely right. I just need a vagina to insert myself into, so I can fulfil a stupid promise I made to myself.

'No! I want to be more than friends,' I lie. 'Always have.' If my mother were here she'd slap me across the face and write me out of her will.

I take Hayley's chin in my hand and kiss her again. This time she reciprocates.

We stand there for a few minutes snogging like the two drunks we are, until Hayley breaks away. 'I've got a Christmas present for you,' she says in a coy tone of voice.

'*Have you?*'

'Yeah. I was going to give it to you later in the week, but as you're here, and we're, you know, getting on so well...' Hayley gives me a shy smile. 'It's in my bedroom,' she says. 'Want to come see it?'

'Yes. Yes I do!'

You loathsome little toad, Matt Bunion. You awful excuse for a human being.

Hayley takes my hand and leads me into her bedroom.

It's a room any self respecting nerd would love. There are Star Trek and Doctor Who posters on the walls, and a variety of figurines, models and other ephemera from the science fiction and fantasy world, on a series of shelves that line every wall in the spaces where there aren't posters. The room is tiny, and made even smaller by the clutter. Hayley has managed to squeeze a small double bed in, along with a bed side table and a wooden chair, but that's about it.

'I haven't wrapped it yet,' she tells me and opens the door in the bedside table. 'And I couldn't find it in the original packaging, but I know you've wanted one for ages, so...' Hayley comes back over to me, one hand held behind her back. 'Close your eyes and hold out your hand.'

I do so and feel her place something small into it. I open my eyes and gasp.

It's the Star Wars character Wicket W. Warrick - Ewok scout and befriender of Princess Leia. Or rather, it's a three inch plastic reproduction of Wicket W. Warwick, made by Kenner toys in 1983 to tie in with the release of Return Of The Jedi.

I've wanted to add this little fella to my collection for years, but have never been able to find one in such good condition.

'Wow, thank you Hayley,' I say with heartfelt appreciation. 'This must have cost you a fair bit.'

Hayley waves a hand. 'Found it on Ebay. Just got lucky I guess.'

—

'It really is a great present.' Certainly better than the Battlestar Galactica DVD I found for her in the Amazon bargain bin last week anyway.

'Glad you like it.' Hayley says, and presses herself against me. 'Now why don't you put it down and kiss me again?'

'Hmmm?' I'm so enraptured by Wicket's goofy little face that I've temporarily forgotten the reason I'm here in the first place. The Ewoks were my favourite characters in Star Wars when I was a child. This is a fact that could get me murdered should it ever come to light at a sci-fi convention. Until Jar Jar Binks came along, they were the most universally hated of all Star Wars characters, for being too bloody cute for their own good.

'Put Wicket down and kiss me Matt!' Hayley insists.

'Okay,' I mumble and turn to put Wicket carefully down onto the chair behind us. I make sure I leave him standing up. It only feels right and proper to do so.

Hayley then proceeds to suck the fillings out of my teeth... at least that's what it feels like.

I have to admire her eagerness. I wouldn't find the prospect of kissing my stupid face to be enticing in the slightest, but Hayley appears to have months of pent-up sexual frustration to work her way through and that means attacking me with almost violent gusto.

She starts to unzip my onesie and perches herself on the end of the bed. 'I want you in my mouth,' she says bluntly, causing me to go bug-eyed in amazement.

I've said before that I will never understand women for as long as I live, and here once again is evidence of that. Hayley has been, for the entire length of our friendship, a really sweet girl to be around. However, she has never struck me as a particularly sexual person. In fact, before tonight I would have bet that she was as much a virgin as I am.

As Hayley yanks down my boxer shorts and inserts my penis into her mouth with the ease and practise of a trained sword swallower, I am forced to rethink my position.

I wasn't expecting this kind of treatment. Nor was little Matt. So much so that he's reaching the point of no return before Hayley has had chance to work up much of a rhythm.

'Er, Hayley... '

Slurp slobber suck.

'I think you'd better...'

Suck slobber slurp.

'You'd better stop otherwise I'm going to...'

Suck suck slobber slobber slurp slurp.

'I'm going to cum before we've even started to...'

Suck slobber slurp slurp slobber suck.

'To have... to have... OH MY GOD!'

Slurp suck slobber suck slurp slobber slobber su -

It hits the back of Hayley's throat like a bullet from a gun. She instantly chokes, and her teeth involuntarily bite down on my twitching penis. With a screech of surprise I buck my hips backwards in order to avoid a swift and painful castration by female nerd.

My legs get tangled in the onesie still gathered around my ankles, and I stumble, falling back onto the chair behind me.

Wicket W. Warrick, Ewok warrior and hero of the resistance against the evil galactic Empire, goes straight up my arse.

The scream that erupts from my mouth can *only* be described as the shriek of a man having a Star Wars action figure forcibly inserted into his rear end. There simply is no other experience in the realm of human existence that can make someone wail so loudly, in such sharp, terrible agony.

I don't remember much about what happened next, including the ride to the hospital. I've blotted it out through sheer force of will.

I seem to remember Hayley trying to remove Wicket with a pair of salad tongs, without much success. The little bugger was stuck fast.

I also remember the long, slow walk down the two flights of stairs to get to street level. Every time I lowered one leg down to the next riser, Wicket would shift around a bit. It felt like the little fucker was digging for gold.

I know a lot of nerds like to claim that George Lucas raped their childhoods by tinkering with the trilogy over the years, but I am the only man in the world who knows what that actually feels like *physically*.

When the taxi pulls up outside Hayley's flat it comes as no surprise that it's being driven by the same guy who dropped me off earlier.

'Christ! Two of you dressed in the same clobber!' he roars, and bellows with laughter.

'Just take us to the hospital please,' Hayley asks, as I painfully crawl onto a back seat that stinks of three day old vomit.

If there is a suitable punishment for trying to take advantage of a friend in order to fulfil your nasty little sexual desires, it must surely be lying face down in the remnants of stale vomit, with an Ewok up your arse, trying its best to burrow a way through to your small intestine.

'What's the nature of your emergency?' says the woman behind the counter at A&E. She has to speak up as we're surrounded by the usual collection of Friday night drunks and maniacs, made even louder and more obnoxious by the amount of Christmas spirit they've imbibed this evening.

Hayley stares blankly at her. I groan and blush a violent red.

'What's your problem guys?' the woman repeats. 'We have to know what's wrong so we can treat you.'

'Er...' Hayley begins. I groan again. 'My friend here has... has something wrong with his bottom.'

'Something wrong with his bottom?'

'Yes. Yes, that's it.'

The woman turns to me. 'What exactly is wrong with it, dear?'

'There's an Ewok up there,' I mumble in a strained voice.

'What?'

'He's up there,' I say and lean forward, putting my elbows on the counter, '...and he won't come out,' I add in a pained half whisper.

The receptionist glares at me in understandable confusion.

Hayley sighs. 'He's got an action figure up his arse and we couldn't get it out on our own. He sat on it accidentally.'

The receptionist's eyebrow shoots up faster than a nuclear firework. 'Accidentally?'

'Yes. *Accidentally*,' Hayley repeats. 'Can we get him treated as soon as possible please?'

To give her some credit, the receptionist manages to fill out all of my details without smiling once. 'Just go and sit over there... ahem... sorry, *stand* over there,' she tells me, 'and you'll be seen to once a nurse becomes available.'

'Thank you,' I reply in a shaky voice, and mince my way uncomfortably over to the waiting area.

I'd like to say that Hayley and I stand out in the crowd, dressed as we are in our Boba Fett onesies, but A&E on the Friday night before Christmas is a place chock to the rafters with the bizarre, freakish and abnormal. So much so, that we actually look almost sane by comparison.

In the hour and thirty five minutes I have to stand and wait to be treated, I see one fat man dressed as a sailor and covered in blood rolled in through the front doors stuck fast in a wheelie bin, two scantily dressed women with their hair inexplicably super-glued together, several random drunks in various stages of undress and carrying a variety of superficial injuries, and a small Indian man who accuses me of being the bastard who murdered his grandfather on a street in Jaipur forty years ago, before he's led away by a kindly psychiatric nurse.

Eventually, I get called over to a curtained off cubicle in the far corner of the department.

'I'll stay here I think,' Hayley says as I go. 'I don't really want to see this.'

'Okay,' I nod in understanding. 'Thanks for sticking around though.'

Hayley gives me an exhausted smile and returns to looking at Facebook on her phone. I hope to Christ she isn't thinking of posting a status update.

I walk slowly across the hospital and open the cubicle curtain... to find a familiar face.

It's the nurse with long dark hair who treated Tara the other night. She looks less harassed now. She *also* looks a lot more attractive than I remember. But then, it's four in the morning and I'm standing in a Boba Fett onesie with an Ewok up my arse, so why wouldn't she?

'Hello,' the nurse says in surprise. 'It's you again.'

I sigh. Of course it is. Why wouldn't it be?

'Hi. I'm really sorry about this,' I apologise and shuffle about nervously.

She looks down at my chart and back up at my face again. I can't tell if the watery look in her eyes is due to tiredness or barely suppressed mirth. 'Yeah... I bet you are,' she says. 'But don't worry about it. This definitely makes a change from stitching up violent drunks. You're almost a welcome breath of fresh air.' She pats the hospital bed beside her. 'Now, why don't you come over here, unzip that thing you're wearing, and lie down on your side?'

'Alright.'

It takes me a few moments to divest myself of the onesie. 'Is there much point in trying to explain how this happened?' I say to the nurse as I lie down.

'Not really, no. Which Ewok is it?'

'Pardon?'

'Which Ewok is it?'

'Wicket. The main one.'

'Oh dear,' she sighs and slips on a pair of latex gloves. 'From defeating Darth Vader to being shoved up your backside. Not much of a reward for your efforts against the Empire is it?'

—

72

'Not really no,' I'm forced to concur.

'Right then, just relax Mr Bunion. That's the most important thing here.'

'That might be easier said than done... and call me Matt.'

'Okay Matt. I'm Christina. Now brace yourself, this is not likely to be the best part of your day.'

Christina is very good it has to be said. I only howl in agony once before Wicket is finally removed from his secret hiding place.

'It's a good job I could grab hold of his little legs,' she says as I pull the onesie back up, 'otherwise we might have had to pull him out using The Force.' Christina waggles her fingers in front of my face. I look like I've sucked a lemon. 'Sorry,' she apologises. 'Couldn't resist.'

'No worries,' I reply mournfully. 'I expect I'll be getting a lot of jokes like that over the coming weeks... months... *years*.'

'Well, you've done no real damage anyway. It'll be a bit painful to sit down for a while, but you haven't ruptured anything. You're quite lucky.'

'You know what Christina? If there was one word I'd use to describe myself tonight, *lucky* would not be it.'

In the cab on the way home though, I am forced to reflect that maybe I have been a *bit* lucky tonight.

Firstly, Wicket's insertion hasn't injured me beyond a sore behind and a very bruised ego. I should be thankful for that. Hayley has also promised never to divulge the circumstances of what happened, something I am eternally grateful for.

More than that though, I feel lucky that my overwhelming stupidity hasn't completely ruined my friendship with her. If things had gone differently, we would have had sex - despite the fact that I don't really fancy her in the slightest. That would have been *awful*.

At least I didn't get to take advantage of her in my drunken stupor, and end up hurting her feelings in the long run. Far better my arse gets broken than her heart.

I would imagine Hayley's passion for me will diminish somewhat after tonight anyway. It's rather hard to hold a candle for a guy once you've stared at his reddened and sore arsehole while trying to yank a plastic action figure out of it with the salad tongs your auntie gave you for your birthday.

For the rest of my life, I will consider this a very powerful lesson learned. If you let your cock come between you and a friend, don't be surprised when you discover there's a nasty surprise coming your way.

From below.

...and Ewok shaped.

Christmas Eve - 1 Day Until Christmas

MERCEDES

Well, there's nothing else for it. I'm going to have to find a prostitute.

No, No. I don't care how pathetic it sounds. This is the level I'm working at now, so it's just best to accept it and move on.

It's less than twenty four hours until the big day and I'm no closer to popping my Yuletide cherry, so I'm going to have to take drastic measures.

I simply have no chance of meeting, wooing and getting into the underwear of another woman before midnight. I could be Casanova's direct descendant and still have trouble doing it. As I'm not the type to use Rohypnol either, I'm well and truly stuck.

Having said that, I'm not sure the pursuit of another girl would be the best way forward for me anyhow. It seems to end in disaster every time I try it.

Having already got friction burns on my penis, and the inability to sit down properly thanks to George Lucas, I figure I'd better quit while I'm behind, or risk further serious injury.

This leaves me with two alternatives.

Either I give up and accept the fact that I will be a virgin for the twenty eighth Christmas in a row, or I go and find a professional to take care of the problem once and for all. At least with a prostitute I can dispense with all the tedious mucking about and get right down to business.

After all, if I had a bad toothache, I'd go see the dentist, wouldn't I? The principal here is just the same.

At least that's what I keep telling myself as I jump in the Golf at 8.30 in the evening on Christmas Eve, and head for St Catherine's Road.

I should be out and about tonight celebrating the festive season with my sister Jessica and her permanently ridiculous husband Jeff, but here I am instead, in the car and headed for the only area of town I know that is likely to contain ladies of easy virtue.

I've never done anything like this before, so I have literally *no* idea how to engage a call girl's services. Do you just waltz up and ask for a price list? Or are you supposed to speak in some sort of code, just in case she's an undercover police officer?

I turn into St Catherine's Road with my palms sweaty and my skin pale. Legend has it that this is the place any red blooded man should come to when seeking the services of a lady of the night.

It certainly looks the kind of street one might find sex on offer for a price - a rather dingy back road at the arse end of town, lined with dirty terraced houses and the odd takeaway thrown in every hundred yards or so. It seems pretty quiet for Christmas Eve, a sure sign that nefarious things are potentially going on behind all those closed doors.

What there is certainly a distinct lack of is anything resembling a prostitute.

I park the car about halfway along the road and look around surreptitiously. The street is empty. It looks like everyone is out and about enjoying Christmas Eve - including the prostitutes. I have no choice but to sit here like a prize plum in the hope that one of them comes along before midnight.

Twenty minutes go by and I start to get very bored.

To alleviate the tedium I take a look at Twitter to see what the world is saying tonight. Not a lot of it is interesting, and is mostly to do with what fun everyone is having not sitting in a car waiting for a prostitute. I even try the hash tag *#waitingforahooker* just to see if anyone else out there is as sad as me, but to no avail.

Do you know how depressing that is? That I can't even find someone on *Twitter* who's stooped as low as me this evening?

I lock the phone with disgust and look up.

There's a woman standing right outside my car window.

My heart races.

I look at her out of the corner of one eye. She's not looking directly at me, but is definitely standing a mere three or four feet away and not moving.

She's not dressed in clothes that necessarily suggest sex is on the cards for the right price. Her hands are rammed into the pockets of a dark blue body warmer, and the long sleeved white polo neck underneath isn't erotic in the slightest. The black leggings she's got on may be quite tight, but they also terminate in a pair of fluffy white Ugg boots, rather ruining any slight sexual excitement to be had by them.

The woman looks about forty, and bored out of her tiny mind. How on Earth can she be a prostitute?

And yet...

Here she is, stood right in front of me and not moving. What possible reason could she have for doing this unless she was interested in my business?

While the potential prostitute is not exactly Scarlett Johansson, she is fairly pleasant to look at, and my eyes stray once again to the tight black leggings.

With a shaking hand I roll down my window.

'Um... hello?' I say.

The woman seemingly notices me for the first time. Her brow creases. 'Alright,' she responds warily.

'Merry Christmas,' I add, trying my best to break the ice.

'You too.'

Hmmm.

This is getting me nowhere. Perhaps I should try the more direct approach?

'How much?' I blurt out.

'Excuse me?'

'How much? For... *stuff*?' Oh my yes, I truly am a man of action.

The woman sneers. 'What the fuck are you on about?'

'Oh God... *you know*? How much for your services?' How much for... *for sex*?'

Her mouth drops open. 'You little pervert!' she spits and points at me.

'What? What? But you're a... *working girl*, aren't you?'

'You think I'm a fucking *prozzie*?'

Oh Christ, I've read this all wrong! She's not a hooker! *But she's standing right by my car!*

'You're standing right by my car!' I wail.

'You dirty little fucker. I'm going to get my husband!' The woman then looks down at my rear wheel for some reason. 'Hurry up and finish Miley, we're getting daddy down here to deal with this scumbag!'

I crane my head out of the car and look down. Right by my wheel is a small Jack Russell Terrier attempting to have what looks like quite a painful shit. I look back at the woman in horror and notice for the first time that a thin black dog lead trails from one body warmer pocket to the constipated Jack Russell's collar.

Oh Jesus H Christ on a very large bicycle.

'I'm sorry!' I squeal and fumble with the keys in the car's ignition.

'You just wait until my husband gets down here!' the deeply offended non-prostitute yells. 'Come on Miley!' She starts to drag the poor dog away, who clearly isn't finished with its business yet, as it leaves a skid mark a good two feet long before finally giving up the fight and getting to its feet.

I floor the accelerator and screech away from the kerb as fast as I can, not giving the irate woman another glance. I can just imagine how large and tattooed her husband is, but have no intention of staying around to meet him in the flesh.

I don't stop the car again until I'm three miles away and back in a brightly lit part of town. I have to park up for a moment outside Iceland just to let my heart rate return to normal.

Well, that went *extraordinarily* well.

I'll be lucky if the mad woman doesn't ring the police and give them a detailed description of the pervert in the rusty Volkswagen Golf.

Then again, St Catherine's Road is famous for all types of criminal activity, so maybe I'm actually quite safe. The woman might not have been a prostitute, but there's every chance she's not a big fan of the local constabulary either, and wouldn't want them poking their noses in her business.

Sadly, my knowledge of the local vice scene has now dried up completely. I have no idea where else to find paid sex. I should probably just give up and go down the pub with my sister - as was the original plan for the evening before I developed this harebrained scheme.

Thinking about Jessica reminds me of her husband Jeff - and I realise that finding a prostitute who can cure me of my virginity might not be entirely off the cards after all.

Jeff is what you might describe as a 'man of the world'. He's ex-Navy, ex-council estate, and soon to be ex-husband if he keeps going the way he has been recently with Jessica.

'He's drinking again,' she told me last month. 'I came downstairs on Sunday morning and found him on the front lawn hugging one of the garden gnomes. His trousers were gone and he had lipstick on.'

This is actually quite tame for Jeff. He once went missing for two days before the police found him naked in a stolen canoe, floating in the middle of a boating lake. *Three hundred miles* away.

It was only the threat of divorce that stopped his wild antics for a couple of years, but from speaking to Jess, it sounds like he's up to his old tricks again.

My own relationship with Jeff has largely consisted of him farting on me.

Wherever and whenever the opportunity arises, Jeff likes to break wind upon my person, preferably in my face. He's done this for years. It got to a point where I could no longer stay at my sister's house.

On one hideously memorable occasion he farted so hard it made my eyelids flutter, and I spent the next twenty minutes with my head over the toilet bowl, retching up everything I'd eaten for the past three days.

I would be a happy man if I never saw Jeff again, to be honest.

However, if there is anyone who can tell me how to find a prostitute, it's my insane brother-in-law.

I take a hopeful breath, start the car again, and head for the centre of town.

Spending Christmas Eve with my older sister in a local watering hole has been a tradition since I was eighteen. Jess and I have always been close, despite the vast differences in our personalities and lifestyles. Our bond as siblings manages to overcome the fact that we have absolutely nothing in common. I am a self-confessed nerd with limited social skills, while Jess has always been the most popular girl in town, and thinks nothing of spending £300 on hair extensions.

'There you are!' she cries with delight, as I push my way towards her through the crowd packed into The Frog And Fiddle pub. As per Christmas tradition, Jessica is dressed as a Christmas Elf. I used to do the same thing so we were a pair - until one unfortunate incident six years ago involving me, three drunk teenagers, and a midnight sprint through the Asda car park to avoid a Yuletide beating.

'Hi Jess, sorry I'm late,' I say to her and look around. 'Where's Jeff?'

'At the bar again, of course,' she replies. 'Here, I got you a Budweiser.' Jess picks the bottle up from the table and gives it to me. 'Stevie, Treacle, Michelle and Bob will be here soon.'

I groan inwardly. Michelle and Bob I can handle. They are relatively normal. Stevie and Treacle on the other hand are the couple from Hell. If it gets to ten o'clock before she's showing everyone her underwear and he's glassing an innocent bystander in the face, it can be considered a good night.

'There you are dipshit!' a voice hollers at me from over the crowd. Jeff the brother-in-law has arrived.

...and doesn't he look resplendent in the Christmas Elf costume I can no longer wear for fear of physical violence?

'We thought you'd never get here!' Jeff yells and claps me on the back so hard it makes my teeth clatter.

'Hi Jeff,' I say and try my best to look happy to see him. I'd better keep on his good side if I'm to get the low down on where the best hookers hang out.

'How's your week been?' Jess asks me, ignoring her husband as he swigs his beer and adjusts the ridiculous green pointy hat perched on his head.

As this is probably not the time to tell my sister that I had a Star Wars action figure inserted into my bottom a few days ago, I shrug and say 'Not bad. Yours?'

'Yeah, alright. Glad Christmas is finally here though!' She takes a swig of her own beer. 'Mum says to be at hers by eleven tomorrow.'

'Gotcha.'

I glance at my watch. It's nine twenty. I now have less than three hours to get the job done!

'Fuck me, the beer's going through me tonight,' Jeff tells us, providing more information than is strictly necessary. 'I'm going for a piss.' He turns and marches off towards the toilets.

This is my chance!

'I need a wee too,' I tell Jess and hand her my beer.

'You've only had a couple of swigs!' she shouts after me as I follow my brother-in-law towards the back of the pub.

I lay in wait for him outside the men's toilet until he reappears with a look of undisguised relief on his face.

'Jeff!' I call as he walks past, making him jump out of his skin.

'Christ! What are you doing hanging around the bogs Matt?' he says, and then smirks. 'Are you looking for business?' Jeff guffaws with hilarity at the brilliance of his own joke.

'Actually, I need your advice about something.'

Jeff immediately looks suspicious. I've never asked his advice about anything. I've never had cause to. About the only thing he could have counselled me on before today is how not to follow through when farting on a loved one's face. 'What's up?' he asks cautiously.

'I need you to help me find something... help me find *someone*.'

'Who?'

'You have to promise you won't tell Jessica...'

'Tell her what dickhead? What do you want?'

I hesitate for a moment with embarrassment, afraid to go any further. But it then occurs to me that I've already fucked a coffee table and played anal hide and seek with Wicket W. Warwick in the pursuit of my mission. Asking my brother-in-law to find me a hooker is mild in comparison.

'Can you help me find a prostitute Jeff?' I say in a rush.

His eyes go wide. 'You what?!'

'A *prostitute*. I really want to get laid tonight and have no other options.' I'm aware of how wretched this sounds, but don't really care.

Jeff looks like he's about to cry and opens his arms wide to me. 'Come here Matt, you little bastard. I'm so proud of you!' He then administers a bear hug that nearly cracks a couple of my ribs. 'I never thought you had it in you.'

'You'll help me then?'

'Of course I will! I'll take you down the casino in Redbridge Street.'

'Will they have prostitutes there?' I ask, rather stunned. It would never have occurred to me to try the casino. I thought all you did in a place like that was throw your money away and fail to look good in a tuxedo.

'Yeah, loads,' Jeff tells me with a waggle of the eyebrows. 'They go where the money is, you see.' He wraps one arm around my head. 'Come on, you horny little sod. Let's give your sister an excuse to leave, and we'll go get you some pussy!' And with that, Jeff is dragging me back across the pub by my head.

As I feel my vertebrae separating, I can't help thinking that this might have been a huge mistake.

To give my brother-in-law some credit, he can spin a convincing lie when he needs to. Right there on the spot he makes up an excuse about finding me an Elf costume to wear for the rest of the evening. 'We'll be the three happy Christmas Elves!' he roars and whacks me on the back again.

'But you'll never find a shop open at this time of night, especially on Christmas Eve!' Jessica protests.

'Relax,' Jeff says. 'I saw a cheap costume in the Tesco Express down the road. It'll be open until ten. That'll do him.'

I can tell Jessica is about to protest more, but as Treacle and Stevie have now arrived and are already plastered, her attention is being diverted by their exploits. 'Get down off the bloody table Treacle! They'll chuck us out!' she moans at her friend.

'We won't be long!' Jeff tells his wife and grabs me around the head again, taking advantage of the distraction.

With my spine now stretched to breaking point, Jeff leads me out of the pub into the cold night air, and in the direction of expensive sexual gratification.

Fifteen minutes later and we're standing in the foyer of The Dorchester Casino.

The casino is contained in a gigantic building at the bottom end of Redbridge Street, and was built by a local Russian businessman who obviously has more money than he knows what to do with. His surname, as far as I can recall from what I've read in the paper, is Antonovich, so quite why the place is called The Dorchester is beyond me. I guess it's an image thing.

To one side of the casino is a neon drenched nightclub called Technis, which is heaving at Christmas Eve capacity. There are already several pools of vomit congealing in the gutters outside, so a good night is obviously being had by all.

Above both casino and nightclub is a six storey block of flats, no doubt accommodating young, thrusting professionals who want to be at the heart of the action twenty four seven. In other words, the kind of people I'd cheerfully walk across three lanes of busy traffic to avoid bumping into on the pavement.

In the casino foyer, there is a handy cash point.

'You'd better draw out three hundred,' Jeff advises. 'Actually, make it four.'

'*Four hundred quid*?' I reply in horror. There goes my Christmas bonus.

'Yeah. You want someone with all her own teeth and a clean bill of health, don't you?'

Oh good grief, what am I *doing*?

I draw out the money and we enter the casino proper, which is inevitably full to bursting point. The smell of money is in the air, as is the slight tang of desperation. The only people who frequent casinos like this are the ones who don't care when they lose a grand on the turn of a card, and those who don't care if they *live* when they lose a grand on the turn of a card.

'The trick to finding a good whore is body language,' Jeff remarks, casting a beady eye around the room. He's removed the elf hat and put on a sensible black leather jacket, so he doesn't look quite as ridiculous now. It still took a bit of fast talking with the bouncer at the door before he let us in though.

'Body language?'

'Yep. It's all about the signals they give off.' Jeff moves forward through the crowd, and as he does he explains the finer points of prostitute identification. 'Find the girl who's on her own. The one dressed to the nines, with a smile on her face that doesn't quite reach her eyes,' he tells me. 'She knows she's surrounded by cretins who can't afford her, and is looking for that one guy who is good for the money...' Jeff cranes his head around. 'Like her for instance!'

He points at a redhead in a slinky black dress sat at the bar in the centre of the casino floor. She's nursing a Martini and looks like she's trying very hard not to yawn. In deference to the holiday season, she's wearing snowflake earrings and has a small piece of silver tinsel wrapped around one elegant wrist as an impromptu bracelet. She is also quite, quite gorgeous.

I'll never be able to afford her in a million years.

'Do we go over and speak to her?' I squeak at Jeff. My palms have gone sweaty and my stomach is churning.

'I think you'd better stay here while I chat to her,' he replies slowly, looking at the terrified expression on my face.

I nod quickly and cross my arms, unable to take my eyes off the redhead's long, tanned legs. I continue to watch as Jeff saunters over and engages her in the kind of easy conversation I will never be able to master. I gulp noisily as the redhead flicks her eyes over at me once while Jeff is conducting the negotiations.

After a couple of minutes, my brother-in-law comes back with a broad smile plastered across his face. 'Four hundred quid it is. Meet her in apartment 503 in the flats above us in fifteen minutes.'

I let out an explosive breath. 'Really?'

'Yep. Her name's Mercedes. At least that's the name she's using tonight. She thought you looked quite cute... if a bit nervous.'

'Blimey. Okay. Er... thanks Jeff.'

'Not a problem bonehead!' He digs me in the ribs. 'Just make me proud, and don't spunk in your jeans the way you did with that Cheryl girl when you were at college.'

My blood runs cold. 'How did you know about that?!'

'Your sister has a big mouth sometimes Matt.' He waves a finger under my nose. 'Let that be a lesson to you. Jessica can't keep a bloody secret to save her life.' He looks at his watch. 'Speaking of which, I'd better get back to the pub. I'll tell her you bumped into one of your geeky little friends, who told you about a sci-fi quiz going on down the road, and you fucked off all excited with them. She'll believe that.'

She will as well. That is the kind of thing I'd do unfortunately.

I look back to the bar where Mercedes was sat, but she's already gone. Prepping herself upstairs for the onslaught, no doubt.

'Hang around here for a few minutes, then go up,' Jeff advises me. 'The entrance to the flats is just around the corner.'

'If you say so.'

'And try not to look so terrified. It's only sex.'

Only sex?

This man clearly has no idea who he's dealing with.

I bid Jeff a worried goodbye and spend the next ten minutes wishing I was at home playing Grand Theft Auto. Before long though, it's time for me to go meet my redheaded lady of the night, so I gird my loins, leave the casino in a hurry, and head up to the fifth floor of the Dorchester Apartments, hoping against hope that all of this effort is going to be worth it.

My finger hovers reluctantly over the doorbell to Flat 503.

This is £400 we're talking about here people...

Also, what I'm about to do is illegal. *Prison sentence* illegal.

But then that bastard voice at the back of my head pipes up again and reminds me that I've come this far. Do I really want to turn tail and head home with my virginity still hung around my neck like an albatross of sexual shame?

I let out a small whimper, swallow hard and hit the doorbell.

...which plays a strained rendition of Jingle Bells at me for a full thirty seconds before Mercedes the redhead opens the door.

'Hi,' she says.

'Merry Christmas,' I reply in a tiny voice. 'It's er... nice to meet you.'

She lifts one exquisitely plucked eyebrow and smiles. 'Don't be so nervous Matt. I don't bite.'

'Okay.' I run my tongue across dry lips and try to smile back. I probably look like a serial killer.

'Come in,' Mercedes says and steps to one side. On legs that feel like jelly I enter her flat, and whatever awaits me within its four walls.

I've seen enough movies and TV shows to have a fair idea of what an expensive prostitute's apartment should look like. Every light bulb should be red, it should smell of something exotic like jasmine or frangipani, and all the furniture should be low, sleek and preferably wipe clean. Also, a little light jazz should be playing in the background to sooth the customers nerves and set the right mood.

Colour me completely surprised then when I walk down the hallway, through into the lounge area... and enter Santa's bloody Grotto.

There are no less than *three* Christmas trees in the room. A large one in the corner by a leather sofa, a small one on the window sill, and another big bugger blocking half of the archway into the kitchen. All of them look like they were decorated by a five year old with ADHD.

Several metric tonnes of tinsel hang from the ceiling. It's a wonder the plaster hasn't been ripped out. I actively have to duck just to make it to the centre of the room without wrapping myself up like a fly in a shiny spider web.

The flat does not smell of jasmine or frangipani. If either flower were present, it would have no chance of competing with the stink of pine needles and fake snow. I have to resist the urge to sneeze.

This is not what I was expecting, and my fear turns to bafflement as Mercedes (or whatever her real name is) joins me in the middle of the living room. 'You like Christmas then?' I ask, in the understatement of the century.

'Yeah, I love it! Have done all my life,' Mercedes replies. 'How about you?'

'It's fine I guess. Nice to get presents, I suppose.'

'I love getting presents!' My new prostitute friend clasps her two expertly manicured hands together in delight. 'And giving them as well of course. That's important too.'

'Of course.'

'Do you have the money Matt?'

'What, for a Christmas present?'

'No, for being with me tonight sweetheart,' Mercedes responds, doing a good job of not sounding too patronising.

'Oh yes. Sorry, I forgot all about it.'

This isn't that surprising really, the glare from the tinsel alone is enough to put anyone off their stride.

I rummage around in my pocket and produce a roll of notes. 'Four hundred as requested.'

Mercedes takes the money from me and puts it on the arm of the sofa. 'Thanks very much,' she says and looks at me with a smoky expression. 'Don't worry Matt, you're definitely going to get your money's worth. You have two hours with me, and they're two hours you're *not* going to forget.'

'Um... brilliant,' I reply. 'Always like to get my money's worth, me. You should see me go when I'm on Ebay.'

Mercedes thankfully chooses to ignore this stupid statement. She runs a hand seductively through her glorious red hair. 'Let's go through to the bedroom, shall we?'

My heart starts to thump again. 'Yeah, okay,' I squeak.

Mercedes leads me out of the living room, along the hallway and into a large master bedroom, which is as decked out with gaudy Christmas rubbish as the lounge.

'Sit on the bed for me,' Mercedes says.

I plonk myself down... and try to ignore the giant plastic Santa Claus night light on the bedside cabinet next to me. Call me a stick in the mud, but when I'm about to have full penetrative sex for the first time, the last thing I want to look at is a cheery, smiling Santa Claus holding a big sack and glowing like a Sellafield sheep.

Mercedes bends down in front of me and puts her arms around my neck. She leans in and I feel her lips brush my ear. 'Why don't you pull my dress up Matt?' she whispers, thus creating the fastest erection in human history.

I take both sides of the tight black dress in either hand and start to pull. The material slides up her thighs to reveal a set of stockings and suspenders that I will remember until my dying day. As I lift the dress higher, Mercedes starts to sway her hips back and forth, and nibbles on my earlobe.

This is the greatest thing that has ever happened to me. I would cheerfully insert the entire cast of Return Of The Jedi up my rectum to have it repeated daily.

'Why don't I put some music on?' the new love of my life suggests.

'Okay Mercedes,' I dribble.

She stands, turns, and with the dress still gathered up around her waist, walks across the bedroom to a tiny Bose stereo sat on a broad chest of drawers. This therefore gives me the chance to get a good look at her bottom... and decide that they can shove the cast of Star Trek up my arse as well if they like.

I lean back on my elbows and watch Mercedes flick the stereo on. I figure some light jazz can't hurt right now. It'll certainly calm me down a bit.

But instead of Miles Davis or John Coltrane, what comes from the stereo is a slow thumping electronic note, married to a sonorous chiming bell. For a second I have no idea what the tune is.

Then Paul Young starts to sing, and everything falls into place.

It's *Do They Know It's Christmas?* by Band Aid.

Mercedes is trying to get me in the mood for some loving with a song about starving African children.

—

95

'You don't mind a bit of Christmas music do you?' she asks me. 'It is Christmas Eve after all, and I *love* listening to all the songs.'

'No... I guess not.' It's actually the last thing I want, but I don't want to break the spell her bottom has cast on me.

Paul Young gives way to Boy George as the redhead starts to gyrate around in front of me.

'You want me to dance for you Matt?' she asks, as George Michael is asking all of us to pray for the malnourished little African children.

'Um... I suppose so,' I answer uncertainly, not entirely sure the juxtaposition is all that appropriate.

Mercedes then starts to dance in a way that makes me temporarily forget all about Bono's clanging chimes of doom. As she runs her hands over her perfectly toned body, I have to confess that I really don't care there won't be snow in Africa this Christmas time.

By the time the whole of the Band Aid ensemble hit the chorus, the dress is off and Mercedes is down to her lingerie.

OH GOOD GOD, HER LINGERIE.

As she dances around in front of me, I want to concentrate on what the expensive prostitute is wearing, I truly do. I want to think about nothing other than the way the black material contrasts wonderfully with her alabaster skin, or the way her breasts are pushed together to form two glorious mounds by the bra, or the way the suspender straps curve magnificently across her bottom.

Sadly Paul Young is back, and reminding me that there are tiny, vulnerable children dying under a burning African sun... and it's putting me off my stride completely.

Instead of being horny, all I'm now feeling is a deep seated guilt that I was born in a hospital in England, and not in a shack somewhere in Mogadishu.

Mercedes is oblivious to my dismay and slides her way over to me, stands between my legs and looks down with a sultry expression on her face. She takes one of my hands and places it on her boob, puts the other on her bottom, and proceeds to writhe around and moan like a snake with toothache.

This is all very well, but we have to feed the world, don't we?

I can sit here all night with a gorgeous red head gyrating around between my open legs, but who is going to *feed the bloody world*?

'Um, Mercedes?'

'Yes baby? You want me to do something?'

'Yeah... can you skip to the next song? Band Aid is putting me off a bit.'

Mercedes stops writhing and pouts at me for a moment. 'If you want,' she sniffs, and leans over to pick up a remote from her bedside cabinet. She holds it over one shoulder and presses a button. Band Aid is instantly and gratifyingly silenced.

That's much better. Now I can concentrate on this amazing woman and get my four hundred quid's wor -

Oh fuck me, no.

The next song has started, and it's worse... oh so much *worse* than Band Aid.

I let out an involuntary sigh of misery as the lyrics kick in.

'Are you hanging up your stocking on the wall?' Noddy Holder sings.

Mercedes lets out a squeak of delight. 'I love this one!' she says and unzips my jeans.

I do not love this one. Not in the slightest. As far as I am concerned there aren't many songs that Mercedes could have put on that would have been a worse alternative to Noddy and his band of Brummie maniacs.

The £200 an hour prostitute plunges her hand into my jeans and starts to have a rummage. She's not writhing around in a sexy manner anymore though. Mercedes has now started to bop about in time to Merry Christmas Everybody.

Just concentrate on what her hand is doing Matt, I tell myself. *Ignore Noddy Holder and just think about what* she's *holding instead.*

I close my eyes and tip my head back, focusing on what's going on between my legs, and not what's pumping out of the stereo speakers.

This seems to do the trick. I can feel my penis achieving a happy state again.

I then make the mistake of opening my eyes and looking back up to see my expensive new friend still twerking her arse up and down in time with the beat.

What really kills my mood good and proper however, is when she starts to sing.

'*So here it is Merry Christmas, everybody's having fun!*' Mercedes wails at the top of her voice. It's a good job she has sex for a living, as her singing voice could strip wallpaper.

I shut my eyes again and focus back on my crotch, willing my brain to block out Noddy once and for all.

For the next few minutes I manage to maintain a half-hearted erection as Mercedes does her thing, but then the grand finale of the song begins and I know what's coming next.

Mercedes has continued to sing pretty much every lyric of Slade's seminal Christmas tune - which has been disconcerting enough, but we all know how Noddy finishes the bloody song, don't we? With a flourish, that's how. We've all sung along to it at parties in a drunken state.

With one hand squeezing my penis painfully Mercedes throws her head back, and alongside Noddy she lets us all know what time of year it is.

'*IT'S CHRISTMASSSSSS!!*' she bellows.

'Oh God!' I moan in anguish.

Mercedes misinterprets this completely. 'You like that Matt? You like it when I sing like that?' she growls and starts to move her hand up and down like a milkmaid on amphetamines.

The song finishes, and I groan again, this time in relief knowing that Noddy has finally shut the fuck up.

Mercedes then pushes my shoulders back, yanks down her underwear in a smooth, practised motion, and straddles me on the bed. 'I want you inside me Matt,' she moans.

At last!

After all my effort.

After all the trouble, expense, embarrassment and pain I've been through.

The moment has truly, *finally* arrived...

Mercedes shudders with pleasure and starts to lower herself down onto my co -

'*The child is a king,*' Cliff Richard sings. '*The carollers sing...*'

Oh please God NO!

'*The old has passed, there's a new beginning...*'

Not Mistletoe and Wine!

ANYTHING but Mistletoe and Wine!

But it has started.

There is *nothing* I can do about it.

Like the oncoming apocalypse, Sir Cliff has arrived - the harbinger of doom in a tweed coat and polo neck.

My erection vanishes in a millisecond. How could it not? This is Cliff Richard we're talking about. It has been scientifically proven time and time again that it is impossible to remain in a state of sexual arousal once Sir Cliff starts to sing.

'What's the matter baby?' Mercedes quizzes me from above.

I can't reply. I'm already crying too much.

'Maybe you just need me to put on a little show?' she offers, as Cliff points out that children like to sing Christian rhyme. I still can't respond. There's every chance my brain has thrown a massive and catastrophic embolism just to get me away from Cliff and his army of god-fearing ankle biters.

Mercedes leans over to her bedside cabinet again, this time opening the drawer. From it she produces a dildo. Not just any dildo either, but a *Christmas themed* dildo. Painted onto its long, smooth surface is the face of Rudolph The Red Nose Reindeer.

This woman is about to insert Rudolph The Red Nosed Reindeer into herself while Cliff Richard orders us to rejoice in the good that we see.

I couldn't be less turned on right now if Mercedes was my bloody mother.

'Watch me baby,' she says. 'Watch what I'm doing.'

I am sweetheart, and frankly I'm finding the whole thing deeply unpleasant.

'Stop,' I mumble quietly. Mercedes doesn't hear me and starts to go at herself in the same way you or I would to unblock a sink. 'Please stop!' I repeat a little louder, and grab her hand before she can impale herself again.

Her brow creases. 'What's the matter?'

'Please... *please* turn off the bloody Cliff Richard song,' I beg her.

Now her expression darkens. She's gone from faked sexual arousal to barely suppressed rage in a split second. 'What's wrong with Cliff Richard?' she demands through gritted teeth.

I'm in such a miserable state that I can't read the obvious danger signs. 'He's fucking *awful*, that's what. How am I supposed to perform with him droning on in the background about logs on the fire and gifts on the tree?'

Mercedes waggles the dildo menacingly in my face. 'You fucking take that back,' she hisses.

'What?'

'Take back what you just said about Cliff!'

This is *unbelievable*. I'm paying this woman £400 to usher me into the ranks of the sexually experienced, and she has the gall to moan at me about my opinion of Cliff Richard?!

'No! I won't take it back,' I snap 'Cliff Richard is bloody *awful*!'

Mercedes snarls and smacks me on the forehead with the dildo.

This is decidedly unpleasant. Not only is it quite hard despite the rubber covering, it is also somewhat... *moist*.

'Oww!' I wail, clasping a hand to my head. 'You bloody maniac!'

'Take back what you said about Cliff!' she screams, and whacks me again.

There may be some men in this world who would gladly pay four hundred quid to let a stunning redhead hit them over the head with a used dildo, but I am not one of them.

I push Mercedes back by the shoulders and she tumbles off my lap down onto the bedroom floor. 'You little shit!' she screeches.

'You're a bloody lunatic!' I shout at her and zip my jeans back up.

'Cliff is a wonderful man!' she bawls. 'He's our nation's favourite!'

'Favourite what? Orange pensioner?' I roar.

'You bastard!' The dildo is thrown at my head with all of the fury Mercedes can unleash. I duck out of the way, and it sails across the bedroom, landing on the floor near the window with a squelch.

I storm out of the bedroom and head back down the hallway.

There's no way I'm leaving here £400 lighter, so I go into the living room and snatch up the roll of money from the sofa.

'Leave that here!' Mercedes screams.

'You're fucking joking aren't you?' I grab a fifty out from the roll and throw it back onto the sofa. 'That's for the striptease! If you think I'm paying any more to listen to Cliff Richard sing a load of bollocks, and get assaulted with a sex toy while it happens, you've got another thing coming!'

I march out of the living room and head for the front door, grabbing the handle as soon as I reach it. This is when Mercedes the redheaded prostitute punches me in the back of the head so hard it makes me head butt the door. The world immediately spins, and I see more stars than you would in the average planetarium.

In my now befuddled state I realise I could actually be in a lot of trouble here...

Not only am I now facing an enraged call girl with a right arm like Audley Harrison, there's every chance she has a pimp around here somewhere, ready and quite willing to break my knee caps if he finds out I haven't paid the full amount for her services.

I wrench the front door open. My vision has gone a bit blurry and I feel unsteady on my feet from the blow to the head, but I know I have to get out of here as fast as possible.

With Mercedes still screaming in my ear from her doorway I take off down the corridor as fast as my wobbly legs will carry me, bursting into the stairwell at the end before she has a chance to put on some clothes and give chase.

With heart pumping and blood racing I reach the ground floor and run straight out into the street. My head whips around in fear, expecting to see a giant and enraged pimp coming at me with a crowbar any second.

I sprint through several streets of Christmas Eve revellers, only slowing down when I've put a good half mile between me and Cliff Richard's biggest fan.

As I stop running, the adrenalin drains from my body and the world starts spinning like I've just mainlined a bottle of vodka in three seconds flat. I feel darkness start to edge into my field of vision, and my legs go out from under me.

I'm only saved a painful and bruising crash to the pavement by the arms of someone strong and swift. As unconsciousness begins to take me I look round into the eyes of Christina the A&E nurse.

'Bloody hell Matt,' she says in disbelief. 'What have you managed to get stuck up your backside this time?'

The world goes black.

Christmas Day

CHRISTINA

I awake in the back of an ambulance. A small crowd has formed around it. Many inebriated faces peer in at me. Most of them look highly amused.

I'm lying on a stretcher with the end racked up so my head and shoulders are more or less upright. My head is thumping, my stomach is churning, and I ache all over. In essence, I have every symptom of a chronic hangover, without the joy of the drinking that comes before it.

I glance at my watch. It reads 12:07am. It is Christmas Day.

I have *failed*.

All I can do is let out a long, tired sigh and rub my eyes.

'That's definitely the sound of a man who's had enough for one night,' Christina says as she climbs into the ambulance and sits next to me.

'You don't know the half of it,' I reply mournfully. 'Where did you come from?'

'I was out with my friends celebrating. I spotted you wobbling around on the spot and thought I'd better come over and help. You're lucky I drew the short straw and had to be designated driver, otherwise I would have probably missed you completely. '

'Thank you,' I tell her gratefully, picturing the imaginary pimp with the crowbar again. 'You probably saved my life.'

'My pleasure.' Christina gives me a long hard look. 'What the hell happened to you this time?'

I open my mouth with a lie on my lips, but then I remember that this is the woman who removed an Ewok from my arse. 'A prostitute donkey-punched me in the back of the head after I insulted Cliff Richard,' I tell her in a matter of fact tone of voice.

Christina's eyes narrow and she examines my blank expression. Then she shakes her head. '*Of course* that's what happened. It's never boring with you, is it Matt?'

'Nope. Never,' I am forced to agree.

A female paramedic jumps into the ambulance with us. 'Good to see you awake Matthew,' she says and sits down next to Christina. 'How are you feeling?'

I consider my answer. 'I've been better,' I finally respond, understating things just a tad.

'Well, your pulse is fine and your pupils are responsive. I think you might have a very slight concussion, but nothing to worry about. Can you get yourself home?'

'I'll drop him off,' Christina interjects. 'The others have buggered off clubbing already, and I don't fancy being the only sober one in the group. I could do with getting home anyway.'

'Great,' the paramedic says. She then gives Christina a sly smile. 'You really are right about his hair Chris. It's all over the bloody shop.'

'Sally!' Christina gasps and goes a flaming shade of red.

She's been talking about me to her work colleagues. Why would she do that?

Sally then peers around at my backside with a smirk. 'He seems to be sitting down without too much trouble. I guess R2-D2 didn't do any permanent damage, eh?'

Christina gasps again, this time in horror.

My mouth drops open. The paramedic knows about what happened the other night!

Alright, she's obviously not a Star Wars fan - it was quite blatantly Wicket W. Warwick, not C3PO's little buddy that went excavating in my colon, but Christina has obviously blabbed about it to her!

How many more of her workmates did this bloody woman regale with the story of the weirdo who had a toy up his bottom?

I feel tears of shame prick my eyes. 'I want to leave now please,' I say quickly, swinging my legs off the stretcher.

'Careful Matt,' Christina warns. 'You're still concussed.' She puts one hand on my arm.

I shrug it off and stand. 'Leave me alone. I want to get out of here before any more of your friends turn up to take the piss out of me.'

I jump down from the ambulance and make my way through what's left of the crowd of onlookers.

'Matt!' I hear Christina cry. 'Come back!'

I ignore her and pound along the pavement. I have no idea where I'm going, I just know I need to get away from that ambulance as quickly as possible.

'Matt! Please! Come back!'

'No!' I shout over my shoulder. Then I change my mind and spin round to confront her. I don't want to leave without giving the blabbermouth nurse a piece of my mind. 'I can't believe you told people what happened to me! I should bloody sue you and the NHS!'

Christina puts her hands up. 'I only told Sally about you! She's one of my best friends.'

'Oh, that makes it okay does it?!' I storm.

'I didn't tell her to take the piss out of you.'

'Really? Then why the fuck would you say anything?'

'Because...' Christina hesitates.

'Because what?!'

'Because I fancied you!'

I'm struck dumb. I can't believe what I've just heard.

Then I remember the circumstances of our first conversation. 'How the hell can you fancy me?' I ask. 'You pulled an Ewok out of my bum!'

Christina rolls her eyes. 'Please Matt. I'm an A&E nurse. I see things every day that would make you throw up, and I have to put up with people acting far worse than you can imagine. A plastic toy and a swollen arsehole aren't likely to put me off, trust me.' She sighs. 'I thought you handled the whole thing very well, actually. I also thought you were cute. Even in the Boba Fett onesie.'

'You thought I was *cute*?'

She rolls her eyes again. 'Yes. I am quite clearly suffering from some kind of severe mental illness, but I thought you were good looking... and I couldn't stop thinking about you after you left that night. That's what I told Sally.'

There are times in life when the rug is completely pulled out from under your feet. This is definitely one of them. Several rugs, in fact. And a shag-pile carpet.

'I don't know what to say,' I tell her in disbelief. 'This all comes as something of a shock, to be honest.'

She laughs. 'Yes. I'm sure it does. It might take a while to sink in, I guess. It's probably not up there with being assaulted by a prostitute though.' Christina draws closer to me and takes one of my limp hands. 'Speaking of which, I think I should get you home, don't you? It's getting late and we both need to go to bed.' She catches the change in my expression. '*Separate* beds, Matt. Don't get ahead of yourself.'

'Okay.' I squeeze her hand slightly. 'Thank you for helping me tonight. And thank you for thinking I'm cute, despite all evidence to the contrary.'

'Not a problem,' Christina says with a smile. She then stands on tip-toe and plants a soft kiss on my lips.

It's a kiss that promises a lot more like it are coming in the near future, and it is quite possibly the nicest thing I have ever experienced.

Christina pulls up outside my flat and walks me to the door. We exchange phone numbers, and she provides me with another one of those heart-stopping kisses, before jumping back in her car and driving away.

As I watch her go, a thought occurs that makes me smile with genuine festive pleasure for the first time.

I set out to lose my virginity this Christmas and failed spectacularly in the effort - but there's every chance that while I was trying, I may have found something *much* more important.

The End

About the author:

Nick Spalding is an author who, try as he might, can't seem to write anything serious. He's worked in the communications industry his entire life, mainly in media and marketing. As talking rubbish for a living can get tiresome (for anyone other than a politician), he thought he'd have a crack at writing comedy fiction - with an agreeable level of success so far, it has to be said. Nick lives in the South of England with his fiancée. He is approaching his forties with the kind of dread usually associated with a trip to the gallows, suffers from the occasional bout of insomnia, and still thinks Batman is cool.

Nick Spalding is one of the top ten bestselling authors in eBook format in 2012.

You can find out more about Nick by following him on Twitter or by reading his blog Spalding's Racket.

Printed in Great Britain
by Amazon